DATE DUE

APR 1 5 2009	
MAY 1 3 2009	
APR 1 8 2013	

the higher power of lucky

the higher

power of lucky

by **susan patron**

with illustrations by **matt phelan**

a richard jackson book
atheneum books for young readers
new york london toronto sydney

Atheneum Books for Young Readers
An imprint of Simon & Schuster Children's Publishing Division
1230 Avenue of the Americas
New York, New York 10020

Book design by Ann Bobco
The text for this book is set in Berkeley.
The illustrations for this book are rendered in pen and ink and pencil.
Manufactured in the United States of America
10 9 8 7 6 5 4
Library of Congress Cataloging-in-Publication Data
Patron, Susan.
The higher power of Lucky/Susan Patron.—1st ed.
    p.   cm.
"A Richard Jackson book."
Summary: Fearing that her legal guardian plans to abandon her
to return to France, ten-year-old aspiring scientist Lucky Trimble
determines to run away while also continuing to seek the Higher
Power that will bring stability to her life.
ISBN-13: 978-1-4169-0194-5
ISBN-10: 1-4169-0194-9
[1. Abandoned children—Fiction. 2. Interpersonal relations—Fiction.
3. Runaways—Fiction.]
I. Title.
PZ7.P27565 Hig 2006
[Fic]—dc22   2005021767

for René

contents

1. eavesdropping

Lucky Trimble crouched in a wedge of shade behind the Dumpster. Her ear near a hole in the paint-chipped wall of Hard Pan's Found Object Wind Chime Museum and Visitor Center, she listened as Short Sammy told the story of how he hit rock bottom. How he quit drinking and found his Higher Power. Short Sammy's story, of all the rock-bottom stories Lucky had heard at twelve-step anonymous meetings—alcoholics, gamblers, smokers, and overeaters—was still her favorite.

Sammy told of the day when he had drunk half a gallon of rum listening to Johnny Cash all morning in his parked '62 Cadillac, then fallen out of the car when he saw a rattlesnake on the passenger seat biting his dog, Roy, on the scrotum.

Lucky balanced herself with a hand above the little hole that Short Sammy's voice was coming out of. With her other hand, she lifted the way-too-curly hair off her neck. She noticed two small black birds nearby, panting like dogs from the heat, their beaks open, their feathers puffed up. She put her ear to the hole because Sammy's voice always got low and soft when he came to the tragical end of the story.

But Short Sammy didn't head right to the good part. To stretch it out and get more suspense going for the big ending, he veered off and told about the old days when he was broke and couldn't afford to buy rum, so he made homemade liquor from cereal box raisins and any kind of fruit he could scrounge up. This was the usual roundabout way he talked, and Lucky had noticed that it made people stay interested, even if the story got quite a bit longer than if someone else had been telling it.

She stood up, her neck and the backs of her knees sweating, and mashed wads of hair up under the edges of her floppy hat. She carefully angled an old lawn chair with frayed webbing into her wedge of shade, and made sure the chair wouldn't break by easing herself onto it. Flies came, the little biting ones; she fanned them away with her plastic dustpan. Heat blasted off the Dumpster.

There was a little silence, except for the wobbly ticking noise of the ceiling fan inside and people shifting in their folding metal chairs. She was pretty sure they had already heard the story of Short Sammy hitting rock bottom before, as she had, and that they loved the pure glory and splendiferousness of it as much as she did—even though it was hard to imagine Short Sammy being drunk. Short Sammy's voice sounded like it could barely stand to say what came next.

"That Roy, man," said Sammy, who called everyone "man,"

even people like Lucky who were not men. "He was one brave dog. He killed that snake even though it bit him in the place where it hurts the worst for a male. And there I am, trying to get away, falling out of the Cad. I break a tooth, I cut my cheek, I give myself a black eye, I even sprain my ankle, but I'm so drunk, man, I don't even know I'm messed up—not till much later. Then I pass out.

"Next day I wake up on the ground, sand in my mouth, and it feels like death. I mean, it's like I *died*, man, but at the same time, like I'm too sick and ashamed to be dead. There's a mangled rattlesnake under the car, there's blood, lots of blood— I don't even know if it's my blood or Roy's or the snake's. Roy's gone. I call him—nothing. I figure maybe after saving my stupid life he went off to die alone somewhere. It's probably like a hundred degrees in the shade, man, about as hot as it is now, but I'm so cold I can't stop shivering."

Lucky's hands smelled metallic, like the thin arms of the lawn chair; they felt sticky. She pushed her hat back from her forehead; air cooled the sweat there.

"I make this deal with myself," Sammy continued. "The deal is if Roy is okay I'll quit drinking, join AA, get clean."

Lucky edged her bare leg away from a rough, poking strand of chair webbing. Each time Short Sammy came to this part in his story, Lucky thought of what kind of deal *she* would make with *her*self if she hit rock bottom. Like, let's say she didn't know if her dog, HMS Beagle, was alive or dead; she would have to do something really hard and drastic as her end of the bargain. Or,

3

let's say that her Guardian just gave up and quit because Lucky did something terrible. The difference between a Guardian and an actual mom is that a mom can't resign. A mom has the job for life. But a Guardian like Brigitte could probably just say, "Well, that's about it for *this* job. I'm going back to France now. *Au revoir.*" There poor Lucky would be, standing alone in the kitchen trailer, at rock bottom. Then she would have to search for her own Higher Power and do a fearless and searching moral inventory of herself, just like Short Sammy and all the other anonymous people had had to do.

Short Sammy went on, "Then my wife drives up. Man, I didn't even know she'd gone. I'm still kind of laying there on the ground. She gets out of her car, but she doesn't say one word about how messed up I am.

"All she says is, 'I took Roy to the vet's in Sierra City.' She's talking real calm, almost like she's not mad or anything. She says, 'Fifty miles from here, and I drove it in, like, maybe half an hour. That was the worst drive of my life, Sammy, thanks to you. But Roy's okay because I got him there in time for the antivenom to work.'

"Then she goes into the house and comes out with her suitcases that she must have packed the night before, and Roy's food dish and water bowl. That killed me, her taking his food dish and water bowl. All she says to me is, 'Don't call me.' *That*, man, was rock bottom. So I threw down the shovel. And here I am."

There was clapping, and Lucky knew that pretty soon they would pass a hat around for people to put money in. It was a little disappointing that today nobody had explained how exactly they had found their Higher Power, which was what Lucky was mainly interested in finding out about.

She didn't get why finding it was so *hard*. The anonymous people often talked about getting control of their lives through their Higher Power. Being ten and a half, Lucky felt like she had no control over her life—partly because she wasn't grown up yet—but that if she found her Higher Power it would guide her in the right direction.

Chairs scraped as everyone stood up. Now they would all say a little prayer together, which Lucky liked because there was no church or synagogue or anything in Hard Pan, California, so the Found Object Wind Chime Museum and Visitor Center was the closest they got to one. That meant the end of the meeting and time for her to disappear quick. She'd finished her job of clearing trash from the patio in front—smashed beer cans and candy wrappers from yesterday's Gamblers Anonymous meeting. It wasn't likely that anyone would be coming back to the Dumpster behind the museum, but someone *might*. She had to hurry, but she had to hurry *slowly*, in order not to make a sound.

She stashed her dustpan and rake beside the wall and left the aluminum lawn chair hidden behind the Dumpster. Tomorrow, Saturday, would be her day off. Then on Sunday afternoon, before the Smokers Anonymous meeting, she would again clean up the museum's little patio. The patio was where the anonymous people sat around talking after their meetings. All the anonymous people left lots of litter, and each group could not bear to see the butts or the cans or the candy wrappers of

the group that met before it. The reason was that they were in recovery. The recovering alcoholics hated to see or smell beer cans left by the recovering smokers and gamblers; the recovering smokers could not stand cigarette butts left by the recovering drinkers, and the recovering overeaters hated to see candy wrappers left by the recovering drinkers, smokers, and gamblers. Which meant that Lucky had a job—a great job—and except for Dot's kitchen-and-back-porch Baubles 'n' Beauty Salon and the Captain's mail-sorting job at the post office, it was the only *paying* job in town.

Wrestling with the straps of her survival kit backpack, which she had with her at all times, then jogging down the dry streambed toward home, Lucky thought of a question that Short Sammy's story had lodged into one of her brain crevices. She figured she had so *many* crevices and wrinkles, almost all of them filled with questions and anxious thoughts, that if you were to take her brain and flatten it out, it would cover a huge space, like maybe a king-size bed.

The question of Short Sammy's dog's scrotum settled into

one certain brain crevice as she picked her way among the weedy bushes of the dry wash. Even though Lucky could ask Short Sammy almost anything and he wouldn't mind, she could never ask about the story of Roy, since she had *overheard* it. If she asked about Roy, then he would know that she'd been eavesdropping at the anonymous twelve-step meetings.

Scrotum sounded to Lucky like something green that comes up when you have the flu and cough too much. It sounded medical and secret, but also important, and Lucky was glad she was a girl and would never have such an aspect as a scrotum to her own body. Deep inside she thought she *would* be interested in *seeing* an actual scrotum. But at the same time—and this is where Lucky's brain was very complicated—she definitely did *not* want to see one.

A little breeze had come up by the time she got home to the half circle of trailers. First was her little shiny aluminum canned-ham trailer, where she and HMS Beagle slept. Next, the long kitchen–dining room–bathroom trailer, and last, Brigitte's Westcraft bedroom trailer. Instead of having wheels and being hooked up to cars to tow them around, the three trailers were mounted on concrete blocks; plus they were anchored to the ground with metal cables to keep from being blown over in windstorms. The best part was that you could walk from Lucky's canned ham to Brigitte's Westcraft without ever going outside, because passageways had been cut where the trailers' ends touched, and sheets of metal had been shaped and soldered together to join all three trailers, so not even a mouse would be able to find a crack or an opening anywhere.

HMS Beagle bounded out from under the kitchen trailer to smell her and find out where she had been. "HMS" stands for "His Majesty's Ship," and the actual original HMS *Beagle* was a beautiful ship that took the scientist Charles Darwin all around the world on exciting discoveries. Lucky's dog—who was neither a ship nor a beagle—got her name because of always being with Lucky on *her* scientific adventures. Also, HMS Beagle was beautiful, with very short brown fur, little dog-eyebrows that moved when she was thinking, and big ear flaps that you could see the veins inside of if you held them up to the light.

A breeze rattled the found object wind chimes at the Found Object Wind Chime Museum and Visitor Center, and the high desert air carried that sound in front of it, all the way across town, down to the three trailers at the very end of Hard Pan. Just the sound of those chimes made Lucky feel cooler. But she still had doubts and anxious questions in all the crevices of her brain, especially about how to find her Higher Power.

If she could only find it, Lucky was pretty sure she'd be able to figure out the difference between the things she could change and the things she couldn't, like in the little prayer of the anonymous people. Because sometimes Lucky wanted to change everything, all the bad things that had happened, and sometimes she wanted everything to stay the same forever.

2. brigitte

Brigitte's old leather sandals were on the step outside the kitchen trailer, which was why HMS Beagle had been waiting in her dug-out hollow underneath. Lucky and HMS Beagle both knew the shoes on the step meant that Brigitte had just mopped the floor and she didn't want sand tracked in by the dog. Inside, Brigitte stood barefoot at the far end, feeding dirty towels into the washer and talking French on the phone.

Lucky dropped her survival kit backpack on the floor by the built-in table; the trailer smelled of Mrs. Murphy's floor wax and hard-boiled eggs and the sprig of wild sage in a little vase over the sink. Brigitte always cleaned floors barefoot. Lucky noticed that Brigitte's feet seemed to be filled with many more bones than other people's feet; she had sharp, jutting-out ankle bones and toes that were almost like fingers.

If Brigitte were ever to have a child, that child's feet would not look at all like Lucky's sturdy, wide feet with their short, stubby toes. That child would also have very good posture, Lucky thought, squaring her hunched-in shoulders. Brigitte turned, pointed to the fridge with her chin, and said, "There is cold tea, *mon choux*; I am talking to my mother." She smiled and shook her head in a tiny, quick way and raised one shoulder, which meant that she promised she'd be off the phone soon.

Yep, Lucky thought as she tossed her hat onto the backpack, already forgetting to work on her posture, probably the thing Brigitte would like most would be to go home to France and have a French baby with bony French feet like her own. She would call her French baby something lovely and tender instead of *mon choux*, which means "my cabbage," or *ma puce*, which means "my flea."

Lucky poured sun tea from a jar into a plastic glass and stood gulping it under the ceiling fan. The great thing about sun

tea is that you don't have to boil water and heat up the whole kitchen to make it—all you do is leave a jar of water with two tea bags in a sunny place. She raked her hair with one hand—hair that felt crusty from sweat and weirdly overcurly from a perm that would take *at least* two weeks to start looking normal. Dot *never* got it to look like the magazine picture. Instead of making it go out at the sides in a wedge, in a very original, cute way like the hair of the girl in the picture, Dot permed and cut it so that it looked like some kind of mushroom-colored garden hedge.

Brigitte laughed into the phone. She poured Tide into

the washer and closed the lid. Lucky knew for a fact that Brigitte's mother was working on a secret, sinister plan to lure Brigitte back to France. Even though Lucky had never met Brigitte's mother, she did not like her one bit; she imagined her as looking like Brigitte but more stringy and tough, with bangs and hair in a barrette at her neck, but the hair gray instead of blond. The mother would never walk on the backs of her shoes or make noises when she sucked ice cubes. She would be strict and formal, like a school principal or the wife of the President of the United States. Lucky stayed directly under the ceiling fan, sucking an ice cube, making slurping noises, and wishing she understood French.

Probably the old mother was right now working on her plot to make Brigitte so sad and lonely that she would go back to France and stop being Lucky's Guardian. She wanted all her grown-up children—Brigitte and her sisters—to live near her in Paris, which Lucky considered very selfish. Lucky was sure the old lady's plan was working, because she sent little packages that made Brigitte cry.

The sad thing in the package last week had been a plastic tube like a toothpaste tube, except with a yellow cap, and instead of Colgate or Crest wording on it there was a beautiful little painting of a picnic basket and a loaf of French bread on a green, grassy place. It turned out to be a tube of mustard. When she opened the package, Brigitte had been sitting at the Formica table. She held the tube in her hand and smiled, but looked sad at the same time. She unscrewed the cap and squeezed a little dab onto her finger and smelled it and tasted it. Then she cried, which Lucky *hated*, and told Lucky it was because it reminded her so much of home.

Lucky sighed, put down the glass, and slid into the dinette seat. Once she finally got off the phone, Brigitte said, "First, *maman* send you a *bisou*, a big kiss, okay? Second, please put your backpack over there beside you on the seat so I do not trip on it." Brigitte unloaded several little Tupperware containers from the fridge. The kitchen trailer was so narrow that she didn't have to take any steps to do this—the counter, sink, stove, and fridge were all reachable from the same spot. "It is too hot to cook, so we have a cold salad for dinner—tuna, eggs, green beans, tomatoes, olives."

Lucky hoisted her backpack off the floor and plopped it beside her on the banquette. "Do we have those olives I like?" she asked. She hated the strong salty wrinkled black ones.

Brigitte surveyed the many glass jars in the door of the fridge. "*Non*," she said. "And it is too bad, because the little olives from Nice would be better, you are right. Sometimes we just have to make it do."

"Make do," Lucky corrected.

Brigitte sighed and nodded. "Make do," she agreed.

3. good and bad

Out of the millions of people in America who might become Lucky's mother if Brigitte went home to France, Lucky wondered about some way to trap and catch the exact right one. She was pretty sure she'd be able to, if only she had a Higher Power.

But when she envisioned her perfect mother, she kept thinking of traits and habits like Brigitte's. *That* always made her think somehow not of the perfect mother but of the perfect *child*, which in most ways Lucky already was, but not in *every* way. Brigitte did not fully realize the ways Lucky was almost perfect, but she did notice thoroughly the ways Lucky was not.

Lucky did not want to speak French, for instance, which is a jumpy language full of sounds that you have to gargle in the back of your throat. The back of Lucky's throat could not learn to make these sounds, no matter how hard it tried. Of course, she had learned to say Brigitte's name the French way— Bree-JEET—instead of the American way, BRIDGE-it.

Lucky got Brigitte as her Guardian when she was eight years old. The reason was that Lucille, Lucky's mother, went outside one morning after a big rainstorm, and she touched some power lines that had blown down in the storm. She touched them with her foot.

In her mind, Lucky worked on a list of good traits and bad traits in mothers.

GOOD

- Keep ToTally alerT for dangers, especially ones caused by sTorms.
- Remember your child needs you To Take care of her, aT leasT unTil she is older, abouT TwenTy-five.
- Pick a husband who will be a solid faTher for your child and can be counTed on To Take over if anyThing bad happens.
- Tell The husband all The wonderful good poinTs abouT The child and make him love her, in case anyThing bad happens.

BAD

- Going ouT in The morning afTer a sTorm in The deserT, no maTTer how beauTiful iT is, especially barefooT.
- Smelling The brand-new clean air and looking up aT The sky To see whaT iT will do nexT, wiThouT paying aTTenTion To dangerous sTuff on The ground.
- Marrying a husband who does noT like children.
- Divorcing The husband.

Some aspects of life are strange or even terrible, but later something okay or even good happens that would never have happened without the bad/strange thing. An example was how long, long ago, a man who later became Lucky's father went to France and got married to a French woman. Then they got divorced because he did not want to have children. Later, that same man came back to America (he was still not Lucky's father yet) and met an artist named Lucille, who had silky-feeling shoulders. This was a thing he probably liked a lot—where you could put your cheek against the top of her arm and your cheek loved that comfortable feeling. Her fingers smelled like paint thinner, a very good smell and Lucky's favorite smell, along with air-conditioned air. Lucille used to hum little tunes for different situations that made you think of certain ads on TV and laugh. So they fell in love and got married.

But he *still* didn't want children, and Lucille divorced him too. It was too late, though. Ha-ha! Lucky was already born.

So when Lucky needed a Guardian to guard her during the time after the storm, Lucky's father called up that first wife, the French one. She was still in France, but she said she would come to California. She came the next day. She turned out to be Brigitte.

15

Only a very big and terrible thing could make her jump on a plane and fly thousands and thousands of miles—because Brigitte did not love Lucky's father any longer, and she didn't even know Lucille, and she'd never even heard of Lucky before. Plus she had her own French life going along, full of plans, and her old French mother. That terrible thing was the thing that happened to Lucille when Lucky was eight, the morning after the storm in the desert.

Lucky loved rainstorms because of how wild and scary

they are, when you are safe inside your trailer with the wind whooshing and blowing like crazy and rain pouring down so hard it turns the dry streambed into a river. Her favorite part was afterward, when it smells like the first day of the history of the world, like creosote and wild sage. The sun comes out and you look around at all the changes the storm has caused: the outside chairs blown away, the Joshua trees plumped up with water, the ground still a little wet.

That is what Lucky imagined her mother was doing—sniffing up the morning and feeling the cool ground with her toes—when she stepped on a downed power line, was electrocuted, and died.

16   And this is how Lucky became a ward, which is the person a Guardian guards. A ward must stay alert, carry a well-equipped survival kit at all times, and watch out for danger signs—because of the strange and terrible and good and bad things that happen when you least expect them to.

4. graffiti

Even though it was only Friday afternoon, and her report on the life cycle of the ant wasn't due until Monday, Lucky got out her notebook, thinking she could finish by dinner. Then Lincoln phoned.

"Hi, Lucky," he said.

"Hey."

Silence. Lucky knew Lincoln had a hard time talking on the phone because he needed both hands for tying knots on a string or a cord. When he was about seven, Lincoln's brain had begun squeezing out a powerful knot-tying secretion that went through his capillaries and made his hands want to tie knots. He'd learned how to tie about a million different ones, plus bends and hitches.

She heard a crash when he dropped the phone and then a jostling while he got it cradled between his ear and his shoulder. This was the usual thing that happened when they called each other.

"Listen," he said. "Do you have any of those thick permanent-marker pens? A black one?"

"I think so. What for?"

"It's that sign Miles asked about, the one he noticed on the way back from school today."

"'Pop. 43'?"

"No, after that. Right when the school bus pulls into Hard Pan."

"Yeah," Lucky said. It was a diamond-shaped orangy-yellow traffic sign. Miles was in kindergarten and was learning to read, which made him interested in finding out what every sign said. Lucky was glad that there were only a few signs on the long highway to and from school in Sierra City. "What about it?"

"I'll explain later. Bring the marker and meet me there in a few minutes."

"This doesn't have anything to do with *Knot News*, does it?" Lincoln got a newsletter every month from the International Guild of Knot Tyers, which he was one of the youngest members of. It was a fairly boring newsletter to Lucky, but Lincoln read every page minutely, like he was memorizing it, and then he told Lucky all about things like what makes a good fid (which is some kind of knotting tool). Lucky knew that the latest *Knot News* had arrived recently.

"Nope," Lincoln said. "It's about the *sign*. Just meet me there. You'll see."

HMS Beagle was already standing at the screen door, looking out. A lot of times she knew what was going to happen even before Lucky did. "Okay," Lucky said, thinking she could also capture a few ants and glue them to her report for extra credit.

She hung up and went to look at herself in the little mirror on the door of the cabinet by her bed. The trouble about Lucky, and this was a big problem she couldn't solve, had to do with being all one color.

Her eyes, skin, and hair, including her wispy straight eyebrows, were all the same color, a color Lucky thought of as sort of sandy or mushroomy. The story she told herself to explain it was that on the day before her birth, the color enzymes were sorting themselves in big vats. Unfortunately, Lucky decided to be born a little ahead of schedule, and the enzymes weren't quite finished sorting—there was only one color-vat ready and the color in that vat was sandy-mushroom. So Lucky got dipped in it, head to toe, there being no time for nice finishing touches like green eyes or black hair, and then, *wham*, she was born and it was too late except for a few freckles.

Before hoisting on her survival kit backpack, Lucky rummaged in it for a small plastic bottle of mineral oil. A remedy she'd thought of to the all-one-color situation, since Brigitte wouldn't let her use actual makeup, was to dab a tiny bit of oil on her eyebrows, which made them glisten so you could at least *see* them.

One side of Lucky's mind wondered if Lincoln noticed her hair-eyes-skin-all-one-sandy/mushroomy-color aspect, but the other side doubted it because he was always absorbed in his knots or in *Knot News*.

Lucky found the marker and her floppy hat, and she and HMS Beagle went outside. Brigitte was watering her big tubs with herbs growing in them.

"This parsley is going already to seed," Brigitte told Lucky. "The seed packet says in hot weather parsley may bolt early. This word makes the parsley sound like a horse running away." She looked at Lucky's hat. "And you are bolting too, right before dinner?"

"I'm meeting Lincoln—he needs to borrow the marker."

"Please come back before the sun goes down, *ma puce*." Brigitte pinched tiny white flowers off of a bushy plant, and Lucky smelled the herb Brigitte put into spaghetti sauce. She said, "I would like to catch that rabbit who eats my basil."

Lucky did not tell Brigitte that it would have been easy to trap the cottontail. She knew Brigitte would skin it and cook it, and Lucky did not want Peter Rabbit for dinner.

She and HMS Beagle set out for the town's main road—five minutes if you took the shortcut behind the old abandoned saloon.

When they got to the sign, Lincoln hadn't arrived yet, so Lucky shrugged out of her backpack and dug around in it for a Ziploc bag. The old rutted blacktop road was too hot to be near—it was much hotter than the sandy ground—so Lucky and HMS Beagle went off to the side by some bushes to look for ants. Pretty soon the Beag found a little lace of shade under a creosote to lie down in, and Lucky found some ants.

As she watched them traveling along in a couple of lanes to and from a quarter-size hole, Lucky had a sudden large revealing thought about ants. At first she felt sorry for them because they were so tiny and could be killed so easily. She could kill ten or twenty at one time, probably. But then she realized that, with ants, it wasn't so much the one individual ant that counted. They all stayed seriously on their jobs and none of them went off on tangents the way people do. For instance, you didn't have one ant deciding to meet a friend and another ant knocking off work early and another ant lying around staring at the clouds.

No, the ants acted like one single machine, instead of zillions of separate tiny minds and bodies. They had good teamwork. If some died, the others didn't stand around worrying about it. For ants, there was definitely no "I" in "team."

So as Lucky was realizing that, to an ant, its Higher Power might be the whole colony *itself*, Lincoln sauntered up. HMS Beagle whapped her tail in the sand, not getting up from her shady spot.

"I was thinking," Lucky said, "about the lives of ants— which is different from the life *cycle* of ants. I mean, think about if some of them die. The others just go on like they didn't even notice. You can't even make an *impression* on them."

"Hmmm," Lincoln said. He held a loop of string between two fingers and threaded one end through it and then back under. Lincoln could be hard to keep a conversation going with. He listened, but he didn't necessarily *contribute*.

"If you were an ant," Lucky went on, "what would your Higher Power be?"

Lincoln scrunched his eyes at her. "No idea," he said, and went to pat HMS Beagle, who stretched out on her back and waved her paws in the air to show him she wanted her chest rubbed. He said to Lucky, "How come your eyebrows are kind of wet?"

Lucky smoothed the mineral oil on her eyebrows with her fingers. "It's a new beauty product," she explained. "For glistening."

HMS Beagle's ribcage looked much more huge when she was lying on her back than when she was standing. Lincoln scratched it. "Your eyebrows really go . . . with the rest of you," he said without looking up.

Lucky didn't have the slightest clue what to say to that. She was pretty sure—but not positive—that it was a compliment. She scooped five or six ants and some sand into the little bag and carefully zipped it closed. "Well," she finally said, "what's the deal with the sign?"

"Did you *read* it?"

Lucky skirted around to the front of the sign, which was bolted to a metal post, and studied the words in large black capital letters against the orangy-yellow background:

SLOW
CHILDREN
AT
PLAY

Lucky frowned. "So?" she asked.

"That sign is about *us*," Lincoln said. "Where's the pen?"

"Lincoln, what are you going to do? It's *illegal* to draw on a traffic sign. It's probably illegal even to touch it." Lucky worried about Lincoln getting in trouble. His mother, who worked part-time as a librarian in Sierra City, wanted him to grow up to be the President of the United States. Lucky knew that if he ran for President, during his campaign his opponent would uncover every single bad thing he'd ever done in his life. Someone would find out that when he was ten years old he graffitied SLOW CHILDREN AT PLAY and Lincoln could lose the election.

Lincoln's father was an Older Dad with a pension—he was twenty-three years older than Lincoln's mom—and looked more like a grandfather than a father. He drove around the desert in his homemade dune buggy searching for historic pieces of barbed wire, and then he sold them on eBay. Lincoln's dad said he shouldn't worry about becoming the President of the United States until he was in college. Lincoln's mom said he should worry about it *every day, starting now.* But the only thing Lincoln actually worried about, he had told Lucky, was how to get enough money to go to the annual convention of the International Guild of Knot Tyers in England, and then how to make his parents agree to let him go.

"Lucky," Lincoln explained, "people see that sign and they think, 'Huh. Slow children. Kids around here aren't too smart.' Or else they think, 'Gosh, these Hard Pan kids don't move too fast. Must be 'cause of the heat.'"

Lucky had never thought of these interpretations. She figured everyone read the sign and thought, *Okay, time to slow* down *because there are children playing.* "And?" she asked.

"Just give me the marker."

Lucky looked around to see if anyone was paying attention. Down at the side of the dirt road that went off the main paved one, a couple of pairs of boots were sticking out from under someone's old VW van. The wearers of the boots were pounding on the van's stomach. She heard the soft hooting calls of an owl who'd woken up early. The little glass observation tower at the Captain's house, where he liked to sit and watch what was going on around town, looked empty—and anyway she knew the heat in it would be too much to bear right now. There were, as usual, no cars on the road. She handed over the marker.

Lincoln put his string in his pocket and rubbed away the dust beside the word SLOW with the hem of his T-shirt. Lucky was afraid he was going to try to fit DOWN next to it, but she knew he couldn't, and it would look bad. The sharp upside-down V of the top of the diamond came too close to SLOW.

But instead Lincoln did something brilliant. Next to SLOW, he drew two neat perfect-size dots, one like a period and the other a little above it. Lucky knew it was a colon and it made the sign mean, "You must drive slow: There are children at play."

"Wow," she said. "That is . . . presidential."

Lincoln rolled his eyes and blushed and handed her the pen. His dark hair flopped over on his forehead in a springy, independent way. It was hair that would do whatever it wanted to, no matter how he combed it. Lucky liked that kind of hair quite a lot.

In one of her brain crevices where she stashed things she wanted to be sure to remember when she grew up, Lucky put the SLOW: CHILDREN AT PLAY episode. If Lincoln did decide to run for President of the United States, Lucky would go on TV and tell everything in exact detail: the misleadingness of the sign, the cleverness of Lincoln, the neatness of his two dots, the happy-endingness of the story. Except she would never tell the very private and lovely part about her glistening eyebrows.

25

5. miles

A good way to kill a bug that you need as a specimen, without smashing or hurting it, is to capture it in a jar or a tin box. You put a little cotton ball dabbed with nail polish remover in with the bug and, presto, it dies.

Very early Saturday morning, when there was still a little leftover coolness from the night before, Lucky borrowed some cotton balls and half a bottle of nail polish remover from Brigitte's medicine cabinet. She was making an inventory of her survival kit backpack, which you have to do regularly to be sure you haven't used up something important for some reason besides actual survival. It was a good time for an inventory, because Brigitte had gone to the Captain's house to pick up this month's U.S. Government Surplus food, and Lucky was glad to be able to check out her supplies in private.

She was starting to spread all her stuff out on the Formica table in the kitchen trailer when she heard a sound like a pig snorting. Then the pig squealed and snorted again. HMS Beagle thumped her tail on the floor and padded to the door.

"I know it's you, Miles," Lucky called through the screen door. She sighed. "Here's the deal. I'll tell you one Olden Days of

Hard Pan story. You don't get to make *any noises*. Then you have to leave."

From outside, Miles said, "Does Brigitte have any extra cookies?"

"How many have you had already?"

Miles stuck his head in. HMS Beagle's head came up to Miles's chin, and the dog was always happy when he visited because she knew she would get plenty of cookie crumbs. Miles was only five, and he was *not* a neat eater, plus he didn't mind when HMS Beagle licked his hands.

"You mean since today started?" he asked.

"Come in and close the screen before the flies get in," said Lucky, cramming her survival stuff back into the backpack. "Yes, how many cookies have you had since you got up this morning?"

Miles had to push HMS Beagle a little bit because she was smelling him very thoroughly.

"Does banana nut bread count?" he asked as he came in, taking tiny steps so as not to touch any of the cracks on the linoleum floor. He dragged a plastic Buy-Mor-Store grocery bag.

"Who gave you banana nut bread? Dot?"

Even though Dot was the bossiest and crabbiest person in Hard Pan, Miles could always mooch a cookie off her.

"Yeah. She said she hoped there would be butter with the free Government food today so she could make new banana nut bread, because her *old* banana nut bread was kind of dry. But I told her I like it dry, so she gave me some and it was pretty good." Miles wiped his grimy hands on his shorts, which were darker on the sides. He took a worn copy of *Are You My Mother?* and a greasy folded paper towel out of the plastic bag.

"I could trade you this for a cookie," he said, unfolding the paper towel on the table. Ever since Lucky had told him he was a mooch, he always offered a trade of some kind. Miles had long eyelashes, big round chocolate-chip eyes, and wavy orangey hair. His fingernails were as dark as if he had been changing the oil in a car. He offered the half-eaten piece of banana nut bread. "It's really good," he said.

"Okay," said Lucky, although it wasn't much of a trade.

Miles said happily, "What kind does Brigitte have? Does she have any mint Milanos? Then will you read me my book?"

Lucky lowered her backpack to the floor and slid out of the banquette. She had read *Are You My Mother?* to him about a thousand times. "Listen, Miles. I already said what the deal is: I'll tell you one Olden Days of Hard Pan story, and no noises from you. I'm not reading that book again. Got it?"

"Yeah," Miles said. "My favorite Olden Days of Hard Pan stories are when Chesterfield the Burro is in them." He folded his lips inside for a second to show he knew she meant business about making noises. Then he said, "She keeps the cookies in that blue box in the cupboard."

Miles had done a thorough cookie-availability check with

everyone in town at one time or another. He was an expert on who had what kind of cookies, who would give him one, and where they stored them. He made his cookie rounds every day.

Dot's Baubles 'n' Beauty Salon was next to Miles's house, so her back door was his first stop of the day. Usually she'd be in her kitchen, where she had her homemade jewelry for sale and her Beauty Salon, with chairs on the back porch for people to sit in while their curlers got dry. Sometimes Miles let Dot wash his hair as a trade for the cookies. If she had a kind he really loved, like mint Milanos, he let her give him a haircut.

Lucky handed Miles a Fig Newton. He ate it in small bites, gently thumping his heels against the banquette. He rested his bare feet on Lucky's survival kit backpack under the table.

"Don't mash my survival kit," Lucky said.

"I won't," he said, and then asked, "What kind of stuff do you have in there?"

"Things you need if you get lost or stuck out in the desert."

"Like what? A map?"

Lucky hadn't thought of having a map before. If you were lost it wouldn't help to have a map, because you didn't know where you were in the first place. "No, like a good book that you can read to not be bored."

Miles nodded. "Like *Are You My Mother?*" he said. "What other stuff—cookies?"

"Uh-uh. You can't keep anything like chocolate, because it melts. You really need things like specimen boxes in case you find some good spiders or insects, plus nail polish remover, mineral oil, and stuff for scientific studies."

"Will Chesterfield the Burro be in the Olden Days of Hard Pan story?"

"Yes," said Lucky. "It happened when Hard Pan was still a mining town, in the century before last. You have to pretend I lived back then, and I was your age, or maybe six."

"I'm five and a half." Miles made a noise like a helicopter.

"No noises, Miles."

"I forgot. Were there dinosaurs in the Olden Days story?"

"No, this was after the dinosaurs. I was teaching HMS Beagle to heel." Hearing her name, HMS Beagle thumped her tail on the floor. "She was still a puppy. We went down the dirt road like if you're going to the old dump"—Lucky gestured to the open desert that began at the edge of their half circle of trailers. Miles looked out the small window toward the purple Coso Mountains hundreds of miles away.

"The Beag wanted to smell *everything*. I remember there was a whole flock of chukars running in front of us—"

Miles made a *chuck-karr chuck-karr chuck-karr* noise, exactly like the birds. He kept doing it until Lucky said, "Yeah, those. You can never catch one because as soon as you get close, they fly a little bit away. But HMS Beagle kept trying, because they're ground birds and can't fly too far at once. The dirt road got to be a little trail, and then we came to the dugouts."

"The old miners' caves? Where I'm not allowed to go?"

"Uh-huh. We thought the caves were a perfect place for our secret home."

"My grandma says they're full of black widow spiders."

"Well, maybe, but we had more important things on our minds. We found this one cave that had an old tin cup and coffee pot and a wooden crate you could sit on, and a little fire pit with a grill. They were still mining silver up the hill and Hard Pan was a boomtown with *hundreds* of people. One day we went up to the mine and I got a job as a dynamiter because I was small enough to crawl into dangerous holes where no one else could fit. You know the reason they call the town Hard Pan?"

Miles shook his head.

"Because the ground is so hard you can't get a shovel in it. It's like *cement*. You have to use dynamite to dig. Well, I became the top dynamiter up at the mine because I could light the fuse and then get out fast before it blew.

"Our dugout was perfect because there was no rent to pay and people left us alone. We had our own burro named Chesterfield that I rode to my job at the mine, and HMS Beagle got to jump on and ride too."

Miles broke off tinier and tinier pieces of Fig Newton, as if he could make the story last as long as he still had some cookie left. "Was Chesterfield a boy or a girl burro?"

"Girl. I once saved her life when she was a filly, so she lived with us in the cave and never tried to run away. She had sweet breath from eating tamarisk blossoms and locust tree flowers, and she politely went away from the cave to go to the bathroom."

Lucky looked up at the arched wooden ceiling of the kitchen trailer and narrowed her eyes, like someone remembering something from long ago. "While I was at work dynamiting for silver in the mine, Chesterfield went to be with the other burros, but she was always waiting for me at five o'clock on the dot when my shift ended.

"But one day a big timber fell on me and I was trapped. I told HMS Beagle, 'Go get Chesterfield, quick, before this fuse blows me to smithereens!' and she ran.

"Well, turns out Chesterfield was way, way out in the desert looking for a special yellow-flowered plant she loves. HMS Beagle had to look everywhere. I lay there squished under the timber, and the other miners were saying prayers because they thought I was a goner for sure. Finally I heard Chesterfield galloping up to the mine. The fuse had this far to go"—Lucky held up her little finger—"before it would get to the end and explode.

"HMS Beagle gave one end of a rope to Chesterfield and ran

into my hole with the other end. She was still small enough to fit, being a puppy. I held my end tight and Chesterfield pulled with her teeth. She pulled and pulled with all her might. Finally I slid out and the Beag and I jumped on Chesterfield's back and we made it safely back to the dugouts. After that I quit my job at the mine even though the big boss owner begged me to come back. Then we lived very happily in our dugout for a long time, until we used up everything in the survival kit and decided to come home."

"Then what happened? Did Chesterfield die?"

"Of course not," said Lucky. "She decided to have a baby burro. So HMS Beagle and I told her it was better to return to the wild and live among her own kind. She's still there, with her husband and child. Sometimes if there is a person in trouble out in the desert, she'll suddenly appear, and if she likes them she'll give them a ride to safety."

Miles held a crumb of Fig Newton in two fingers. He gazed just beyond Lucky. Finally he whispered, "Would she let *me* ride her?"

"She *might*," said Lucky.

Miles blinked, looked at the last crumb, and slowly licked it from his fingers. He wiped his hands on the sides of his pants. "Could you read me *Are You My Mother?* now?"

"No! The deal was one Olden Days story, plus you got a cookie. Time to go." Lucky clomped to the screen door and opened it.

Miles put his head down on the table. "I *traded* you for the cookie," he said in a tragic, muffled voice.

"Out, Miles."

Very slowly, as if his head were made of heavy metal, Miles looked up. There was a little oval of sweat on the Formica where his head had been. He gave Lucky the same exact look as HMS Beagle when she wanted a piece of bacon. "Could you just read the part about the Snort?"

Lucky had a little place in her heart where there was a meanness gland. The meanness gland got active sometimes when Miles was around. She knew that *he* knew he had to do what Lucky wanted, because if he didn't, she'd *never* be nice to him. Sometimes, with that meanness gland working, Lucky *liked* being mean to Miles.

"No," she said. Miles's head fell back onto the table.

"*Chuck-karr, chuck-karr, chuck-karr,*" he warbled, a lost wild baby bird. Lucky noticed how small the thumb-sized hollow was at the back of his neck. "Please, please, please," he moaned, "tell me the story of how Brigitte came to Hard Pan."

As Brigitte's Jeep pulled up outside, Lucky said, "Oh, get Brigitte to tell you." When he looked up with his whole face filled with gladness, Lucky's meanness gland felt better, like a heavy timber had rolled off it.

6. how brigitte came

Brigitte swung up the steps to the kitchen trailer carrying two plastic sacks full of Government Surplus commodities. "Even though it is only eight o'clock, I do not want to see the *temperature* in centigrade," she said. "If I see it only in Fahrenheit I am not so shocked—I do not let myself know what it really means. Miles, do you want to wash your hands?"

"No, thank you," said Miles. Lucky watched as Brigitte pulled Government food out of the sacks: canned pork, canned apricots, butter, and a chunk of something orange.

"What's this stuff? Cheese?" she asked, picking up the orangey brick-shaped thing packaged in a waxed box like a milk carton. It said UNITED STATES DEPARTMENT OF AGRICULTURE on the wrapping. It felt soft.

The last Saturday of the month, free Government food got delivered to the town. You only received free Government food if you had quite a small amount of money. If you had too much money, they wouldn't give any food to you. Most people in Hard Pan didn't have regular jobs, and maybe they got a check every month out of having a disability or being old or from fathers who didn't like children, but it wasn't very much. Most everyone in Hard Pan qualified for the free food.

"We will see," said Brigitte, slitting the carton with a small knife. She sniffed the cheese. Lucky leaned in and smelled it too. Usually the kind of cheese that Brigitte loved smelled like dirty socks and had to be tightly wound in Saran Wrap so it didn't smell up the whole fridge. This cheese had no smell at all.

"I do not know about this cheese," said Brigitte, frowning. She cut off a small corner and held it out to HMS Beagle. HMS Beagle stretched her neck forward, her black nose almost touching the piece of cheese. She studied it with her nose twitching, then sighed and turned back to her place by the door.

Brigitte made a *pfff* sound, a little blast of air, and tossed the small corner of cheese in the garbage can.

"No wonder it is free, that cheese," she said. "No one will pay for it."

Miles began pounding his heels against the banquette. "Lucky said you would tell me the story of how you came to Hard Pan to take care of her," he said.

Brigitte shrugged. "You know already, Miles. I come on the airplane after Lucky's mother died."

"Why didn't Lucky's father take care of her himself?" asked Miles.

Brigitte poofed air out of her mouth in a way she did to show she thought something was ridiculous. "He is," she said, "in some ways, a very foolish man, Lucky's father."

Miles looked at Lucky to see if she agreed with this or not. Lucky stuck her face closer to his and made big-eyes at him as a way of telling him to shut up. Miles stuck *his* face out and made big-eyes back at her as a way of saying he *still* wanted to know if Lucky agreed that her father was foolish.

Lucky said, "So my father called up his first wife, who he was married to before he got married to my mother. And guess who that was?"

Miles stared at her. "Who?" he said.

"Brigitte!" said Lucky.

"*Her?*" asked Miles. He turned to Brigitte, hugging his Buy-Mor-Store bag to his chest. He frowned at her and then at Lucky to show he didn't want to be teased.

"Of course, me," said Brigitte. She glanced up at a shiny metal thing like a vase on a high shelf. Lucky knew what was in it, but her mind did not like to stay thinking about it. Her brain went hopping off, like someone crossing a stream by jumping from stone to stone, quickly, so they wouldn't have time to think about slipping and falling into the water.

"If Brigitte was married to Lucky's father, then she is Lucky's stepmother," Miles said.

Lucky felt a little bit hypnotized, as if she were apart from her self and the self leaning on the sink was a totally other self. "No," she said slowly. "Because they were married *before.*"

"Lucky's father and I were married before Lucky was born, Miles," Brigitte explained. "Her mother, Lucille, and I did not

know one another. But Lucky's father called me because he knew I would come." She shrugged. "In France I have no job. Always I want to see California. He knew I will take care of Lucky for a while.

"So I agree. I say to him, 'You buy me the ticket and I will come.' 'I have already the flight booked,' he said. 'You leave Paris tonight and arrive in Los Angeles tomorrow.' So I fly to Los Angeles with my red silk dress and high-heeled shoes and only my one little suitcase."

"What happened when you got to Los Angeles?" Miles asked. Lucky knew that Miles thought L.A. was a terrible place where people drove around in their cars all day, from morning to night. He and Short Sammy spent hours listening to L.A. traffic reports on the radio.

"Lucky's father has rented a big American car that is waiting for me at the airport," Brigitte said. "I drive and drive and drive and finally the city ends and the desert starts. Then I drive and drive and drive"—Brigitte air-drove a car, her hands gripping a pretend steering wheel—"until there is no more people, only desert, a *lot* of desert! I am a little frightened because there is too much space everywhere, and I almost drive into a cow and her little veal. . . ."

"Her little *calf*," Lucky said.

"Yes, the cow and her little calf. They are in the middle of the highway! Finally I drive until there is no more road, only dirt streets. There is a little sign, 'Hard Pan, Pop. 43,' and I am sad because Lucky's *maman* has died, so now it is Pop. 42."

They never changed the sign, though, Lucky realized. But because Brigitte came, it was still a true sign after all.

Brigitte squeezed into the banquette next to Miles.

"Did you find Lucky then?"

"No. When I get out of the car I see that it is very, very hot—as hot as today, but I had not ever been so hot in France." Brigitte told the story in her excited French way, which was a way, Lucky thought, that made people listen more thoroughly. "So I go up to this house and it has a glass tower on the roof. I do not know it is the Captain's house, of course. I do not know any person in America except Lucky's father, who is in San Francisco. I am afraid to speak bad English,  so I do not know what will happen. The man at the door has long gray hair and he is wearing some kind of big shirt with a rope for the waist. His dusty leather sandals and his beard make him seem like a person from the Bible."

"The Captain doesn't look from the Bible," said Miles. "He looks normal."

"To me, my first day in America, he looks actually like

someone who has lost his marble. Later, I discover how nice he is, when he drives us back from Sierra City in his van after we return the rental car."

"Don't they have people like the Captain in France?" asked Miles.

"Not exactly," said Brigitte. "Next what happens is I say, 'Lucky?' and I explain everything in French, but he does not understand. Then he says, 'Oh! Oh! LUCK-y!' because I have been saying this name with my accent the way I did before, 'LU-key.' Then he takes me up the hill to an old metal tank with a door in the front."

"Short Sammy's water tank!" Miles said.

"Yes, and Sammy comes out, but I do not know who he is. I see a tiny man with a hat like a cowboy—but a miniature cowboy. I think, no one has told me America is so strange."

Lucky remembered this part brilliantly because she had been there, peering out from inside Sammy's water tank house. Her first sight of Brigitte reminded Lucky of the beautiful ladies on Short Sammy's calendar. Every month there was a different lady, looking very sparkly and smiley, and not wearing too many clothes. Brigitte's dress fit her more like a bright red slip, except the twirly skirt gave you thoughts of dancing. Plus her blond hair was shiny and bouncy, and her lipstick was the perfect, exact same red as her dress. Her high-heeled shoes and creamy clean neck made Brigitte look way too French, and too . . . fancy for Hard Pan.

But the thing she remembered most strongly was that something bad to do with her mother had happened and she was at Short Sammy's and her mother wasn't there.

"Did Lucky know you were her Guardian?" Miles asked, smoothing the plastic of his Buy-Mor-Store bag, as if soothing a cat.

"No," said Lucky. "She wasn't, yet."

"I was going only to stay a short while," Brigitte explained. "Just until Lucky can be placed in a foster home. I promise her father that. I tell him that I must go home to France after." Brigitte fanned herself with a piece of the waxed cheese carton.

Miles asked, "Was I born yet?"

"Yes," said Brigitte. "You were a fat little boy of three years old then, almost a wild child, running everywhere in the town. Your grandmother is always looking for you." Brigitte shrugged. "I try to understand American customs, but they are so different from mine. And Lucky for a long time cannot sleep unless I am with her. She is of course very sad and missing her *maman*."

"Was I allowed to do anything I wanted?" asked Miles. He tucked the plastic sack tightly around his book.

"I thought it was perhaps the way of all American children to be so free," Brigitte said. "I wanted Lucky to have a good American foster family who is letting her be a little bit free and also giving her some discipline."

"Will Lucky have to go to a foster family where they make her take care of all the other little foster brothers and sisters?"

Miles had asked Lucky about this before. It was something he had seen on a TV program.

"For a long time we cannot find *any* foster family for Lucky. Then her father tells me all the paperwork for California will be easier if I become her Guardian, especially because Lucky and I, we have already the same last name of Trimble. I say okay." Brigitte got up and continued to put the Government Surplus food away, frowning at the canned pork.

Lucky was thinking that even though Brigitte said okay, she meant only until they *did* find a foster family. And if she had to take care of all the crying orphaned babies in her new foster family, that would mean leaving Hard Pan. Then the sign that still said POP. 43 would really be wrong.

But what Lucky wanted most was for that sign to stay the same forever, with no subtracting allowed.

7. tarantula hawk wasp

After Miles left, while Brigitte went through a stack of bills to take to the post office later, Lucky thought hard about how to keep from having to go away and live with a foster family. Maybe if Brigitte realized that one day Lucky would become a world-famous scientist like Charles Darwin, she would stop missing France all the time. She would have the extreme glory of being a world-famous scientist's Guardian.

Before she could become a *world*-famous scientist, Lucky needed to turn herself into a famous *Hard Pan* scientist, and the way to do that was to get lots of people to come to the Found Object Wind Chime Museum and Visitor Center. It was her job of cleaning its patio that had given Lucky a brilliant museum-improvement idea. The problem was that it wasn't museumy *enough*. It was just glass cases against the walls with old mining equipment and old photos and a few old bugs, but not enough bugs or birds. Plus you couldn't lean on the glass cases, which you needed to do in order to get a really good close look.

Lucky's idea was that, even before she became *really* famous, people in other countries, and especially in France, would hear about the museum's amazing new scientific display—Lucky already envisioned the display exactly—and they could come for a visit. Brigitte could talk French to them and explain that it was actually *her ward* (meaning Lucky herself) who had made the display. All the French mothers would wish *they* had wards like Lucky.

The timing to work on her secret museum-display idea was perfect, because at ten o'clock everyone in Hard Pan went to the post office for their mail. Since there was no market or restaurant or even a gas station in Hard Pan, people liked to stand around getting the latest news in town while they waited for the Captain to distribute the mail into each P.O. box. So Brigitte would be gone for at least half an hour, enough time for Lucky to get a good start on her display.

She was in her canned-ham trailer gathering her specimens together when Brigitte called from the connecting kitchen trailer.

"Did you put all your dirty clothes in the machine, Lucky? I am starting a wash."

"Yeah, everything."

"Can you listen for the end of the cycle and put the clothes in the dryer if I'm not back yet from the post office? I want these towels to have the California softness."

"Okay." California softness was Brigitte's way of saying fluffy, dried-in-the-dryer towels, as opposed to straight, crispy, hung-on-the-clothesline towels.

"Do not forget, please, Lucky. I have to do the sheets after."

"'Kay."

After Lucky heard the screen door slam and the Jeep start, she carried everything for her project to the Formica table in the kitchen. She wasn't supposed to work on her specimens at the table, but she needed to spread out. And anyway, she'd be done by the time Brigitte got back.

The collection of specimens, taken out of their Altoid boxes and lined up in a row, was magnificent. She had a hoverfly (waspy looking), two craneflies (mosquitoey looking), a giant tarantula hawk wasp, and a delicate baby scorpion.

Lucky measured the wasp specimen head to tail. It was almost an inch long, a beauty with big, orange wings. The first time you see one may be alarming when it zooms around diving-bombing at you. Brigitte was afraid of them, even though Lucky had explained that they mostly wouldn't hurt people. All they wanted was a nice fat tarantula.

Lucky began writing the description that would be put in the museum case. It needed to be both dramatic *and* scientific. She wrote:

The Story of Tarantula Hawk Wasps
and Their Victems The Tarantulas

DO NOT READ ALOUD TO VERY YOUNG CHILDREN

1. The main job of The TARANTULA HAWK WASP is To find a Tarantula and sting iT beTween iTs legs. By The way even Though These wasps are preTty

big and scary looking, don't worry. Human beings
are a Total waste of Their Time.
2. Finally The TARANTULA HAWK WASP finds a
Tarantula. This is preTTy easy in The fall, when all
The Tarantulas walk across The main road

Lucky stopped to think about this for a moment. She had
not yet discovered *why* the tarantulas were all traveling south-
west in the fall, and she thought it would be interesting to
include this information. She thought the museum visitors who
came from around the world would want the complete story.
Later she would ask Short Sammy, but for now she wrote:

buT no one knows why, unforTunaTely.
3. Then There is a big fighT! The TaranTula Tries
hard To geT away. The wasp wins The fighT, she is
happy because now she can lay her egg which is
her mosT imporTanT duTy.

WARNING: THE NEXT PART IS GRUSOME

4. The TARANTULA HAWK WASP sTings The
TaranTula, who becomes paralized buT noT dead.
Then The TARANTULA HAWK WASP digs a hole,
a GRAVE for The TaranTula, and lays her egg inside
The TaranTula's acTual STILL ALIVE body. When
The egg haTches, iT isn'T a flying wasp yeT. IT is
only a grub. BuT iT is very hungry and guess whaT
iT eaTs? The TaranTula!

Lucky was very pleased with the story, which was thrill-ing and horrid. The tourists and visitors to the Visitor Center would say, "That little town of Hard Pan has quite a wonderful museum. I wonder who made that interesting exhibit?" And they'd say, "I sure never thought I'd feel sorry for a *tarantula!*" Lucky was picturing large groups of them gathered around the bugs' dusty glass case, peering excitedly at the tarantula hawk wasp, when Brigitte pulled open the screen door.

8. snake

Too late to hide the specimens. Lucky scooped them into their boxes, which you have to be very careful about or their legs or wings break off, but Brigitte had already seen. Instead of acting mad and making Lucky scrub the entire table with Ajax—not just the little place where the specimens had actually touched it—Brigitte went to the sink and leaned on it, gazing out the window.

"Oh, Lucky," she said, "bugs again on the table."

Lucky noticed that the envelope in Brigitte's hand was from her own father. She had recognized his handwriting. Every month he sent a check, but never a letter, even though every month Lucky still thought he might. She said, "Did my father send a letter to me?"

Brigitte sighed. She kept on staring out the window. "No, only the little check that is never enough." She looked like a beautiful daytime TV lady doctor in her pale green hospital scrubs from the Sierra City Thrift Store.

"I have twelve dollars and fifty-six cents saved from my job at the Found Object Wind Chime Museum," Lucky offered. "We can add that to the money he sent."

Brigitte answered by lifting a shoulder and poofing air, her way of saying, "Forget it."

The phone rang just as Lucky realized she hadn't put the wet clothes in the dryer. It was Lincoln.

"Hold on," Lucky told him. Then to Brigitte, "I forgot about the laundry. I'll do it in a sec."

"No," said Brigitte in a faraway voice, a voice that was thinking of other things. She slid a cassette into the tape player, the one with the French songs that Brigitte knew every word of by heart. "It does not matter," she said. "I do it."

"What's up?" Lucky said into the phone.

"Nothing. Why?" Lincoln was not a good conversationalist.

"Lincoln, *you* called *me.*"

"Oh! Right. It's commodities day."

49

"I know. We already got ours. There's some weird orange cheese this time." Lucky could hear Lincoln adjusting the phone. She knew he was tying a knot.

Lincoln said, "Want to meet up at Short Sammy's in a while?" Lucky and Lincoln liked to see how Sammy cooked the free Government food. He had a very unique way of cooking, and he liked having company.

"Okay. First I have to scrub the table because of the scorpion, flies, and tarantula hawk wasp that I—" She broke off just as Brigitte screamed and slammed the dryer door shut.

"Hang on, Lincoln," Lucky said and dropped the phone. In a second Brigitte flew by, grabbing Lucky's hand. She ran outside, pulling Lucky after her. HMS Beagle followed excitedly.

"What happened?" Lucky asked.

Brigitte's eyes were huge and her face was red. She seemed to be sending off waves of heat in the bright sunlight.

"What happened," Brigitte said breathlessly, "is that a *snake*"—she said the word "snake" like most people would say "rotting dead pus-filled rat"—"a *snake* is in the dryer." Brigitte pointed dramatically toward the laundry area at the end of the kitchen trailer.

In a very calm and relaxed way, to show Brigitte that snakes were actually clean and not repulsive, Lucky said, "I see, a snake's in the dryer." She said it like snakes in dryers were not a very big deal. She leaned casually against the aluminum side of the trailer. "What kind of snake?"

Brigitte pressed the heels of her hands against her eyes. "A *giant* snake!" she said.

Brigitte didn't even like to see *pictures* of snakes, which was really, really silly as far as Lucky was concerned, because a picture couldn't hurt anyone. But Lucky knew that to Brigitte an *actual snake in the dryer* was a quadruple gazillion times worse than a picture.

Lucky ran back inside, with Brigitte behind her.

"Do not open the door of the dryer!" Brigitte shouted. "She is in there!"

"Who?"

"The viper! I think she snuck inside the trailer and climbed up into the dryer!" Brigitte's hand and arm showed a snake slithering toward the dryer. "We have to seal it so she cannot escape. Quick—get that sticky gray tape."

"Well, what kind of snake is it?" Lucky asked again.

"I am sure she is a viper—a rattlesnake! Imagine to live in a place where just by doing the laundry you can be killed!"

Privately, Lucky admired snakes because they were very, very highly adapted to their habitat. One amazing true fact she had read was that snakes actually started out as creatures with legs but evolved to *not* having legs because they could move around better without them. In fact, Lucky figured the average person went around thinking, *Those poor snakes sure have been waiting a long time to evolve some legs.* She would never have guessed *not* having legs would be better than having them.

But she doubted that Brigitte knew enough about snakes to tell whether it was a rattlesnake or some harmless kind.

Lucky said, "Brigitte, what does it look like? What color?"

Brigitte shrugged and looked insulted, as if the question had a completely obvious answer. She said, "She is the color of a snake."

Lucky sighed. "What shape is its head?"

A lot of times when Brigitte didn't know the answer to something, either she acted like it was a dumb question, or she *pretended* to know the answer, or else she veered around with an answer that wasn't really an answer at all. "Lucky, we will look at the shape of her head after she has died—when it is safe."

"You mean when it dies of old age?" Lucky couldn't believe how weird *that* plan was. "That could probably take *years*. We'll have to hang up the wet laundry outside and the towels won't have California softness."

"Lucky," said Brigitte, crossing her arms in front of her chest. "Please go get that gray sticky tape right now."

"Wait—yikes. I left Lincoln on the phone. Be right back."

Lucky picked up the phone. "There's a snake in the dryer," she said.

"Miles's grandmother had one in her dryer once. It came in through the vent going to the outside of the mobile home."

"What did she do?"

"Thirty minutes on 'normal cycle.'"

"You're kidding!"

There was a little silence on Lincoln's end. "No," he said. "That's what she did. Her dryer doesn't have a see-through door. Does yours?"

"No, it's just pure metal. So what?"

"She couldn't be sure it wasn't a rattler, so she killed it."

"Brigitte wants to duct-tape the dryer door shut and wait till the snake dies of old age. After that she'll probably want to duct-tape the whole entire outside of the trailers."

Lincoln said, "We could catch a mouse and use it as bait to lure the snake out."

All of Lincoln's plans were both simple and complicated. They were tempting, but at the same time they made you feel doubtful before you even got started. But Lucky now had her own idea. "I'll meet you at Short Sammy's in about half an hour," she said, and hung up. She went back to the laundry area with the duct tape and a pair of scissors and gave them to Brigitte.

Brigitte stuck the end of the duct tape on one edge of the dryer, pressing it hard, peeling off more tape and pressing it against the metal, until she had the door very securely fixed. No creature inside the dryer could get out through that door.

Lucky climbed up on top of the dryer, where she could peer out a tiny window.

"What are you doing, Lucky?" Brigitte asked. She was wearing a don't-you-dare-touch-the-duct-tape-on-the-dryer-door look.

"Wait a sec," said Lucky. Still peering out the window, she stomped the heel of her shoe on the dryer. She braced herself against the wall and banged her shoe on the front and the sides of the dryer. Brigitte watched, but one of the good things about her was that she didn't act like she was the total boss of everything. Especially when it came to the way things worked in Hard Pan versus the way things worked in France, Brigitte was willing to listen to what Lucky had to say.

Pretty soon, through the dusty window, Lucky could see the snake gliding away from the trailer. "It's gone!" she said. She jumped down and dashed outside in time to see its long, thin, reddish, legless, rattle-less body disappear in the dry wash. It was a beauty—about five feet long, thin as a hose. Lucky thought it was a red racer, the kind of snake that eats rats and even fights rattlesnakes.

Lucky felt very wonderful about her Heroic Deed of figuring out how to chase the snake away without killing it in a gruesome way or waiting for it to die of old age. Plus, if it *had* been a rattlesnake, nobody got bitten. She went inside, thinking she had to figure out some kind of screen to put on the vent to keep the snake from coming back. At that moment Lucky knew she was a highly evolved human being.

But Brigitte was at the bathroom cupboard, rummaging through the aspirin and Q-tips and hair conditioner. "Now I cannot find the fingernail polish remover! It is the only way to get off that sticky mess of duct tape!" she said. "It is *wrong* to have snakes in dryers! This is not something that would *ever* happen in France. California is not a civilized country!"

Lucky didn't say a word. It was too hopeless and disappointing. Brigitte hated bugs and she hated snakes and she thought California was a *country*. Plus the checks from her father were too small.

The sad and beautiful French songs played on and on, the sound drifting out the window and into the dry desert air. Lucky didn't know what the words meant, but she understood that Hard Pan was pushing Brigitte away, and France was calling her home.

9. short sammy's

You could smell Short Sammy's water tank house before you got there, because whatever he cooked in his big black cast-iron pan, he cooked in grease. Beans, pancakes, lettuce, apples—always cooked in grease, bacon grease being his most favorite. The smell of the water tank house activated Lucky's hunger gland.

Lucky and HMS Beagle walked up Short Sammy's path, which was not the kind of path you could stray from because it had old car tires along each side, and each tire had a cactus growing in its center, which made sure you went carefully along straight ahead because your feet were entirely positive of the way with a path like that.

The house had once been a giant metal water tank until it sprang too many holes and the town bought another one. Sammy got the old one to live in, one big round room with four windows cut out. The door had been sawn out a little unevenly and was hinged with strips of leather. There was no lock on the door, because Short Sammy wasn't worried about anyone steal-ing anything except his big black cast-iron frying pan, which was the most valuable thing he owned.

Lucky thought that Short Sammy's water tank house was

even better as a house than regular houses, because inside you didn't have the normal impression of straightness and square-ness and corners, or of different rooms. Instead it was a very convenient one-room house with a bed, a woodstove where Short Sammy did his winter cooking, a round table, three chairs, a crate full of books with his guitar on top, and nails sticking out on the wall where he hung a calendar, his clothes, and three stained white cowboy hats. He stored some other stuff, like his official Adopt-a-Highway equipment—orange vest, hard hat, and trash bags—in the big trunk of his '62 Cadillac.

There was only one picture on the wall—a photograph of a goofy-looking dog's smiling face that had been exactly fitted into a clean sardine can. The edges of the can made a perfect tiny frame that also looked a little bit like a shrine. Lucky knew it was a snapshot of Sammy's dog, Roy, who because he didn't die from a rattlesnake bite got Sammy to quit drinking.

The floor was made of flat rocks fitted neatly like pieces in a puzzle, with concrete poured into the cracks—it was a floor you could spill things on and not worry. Short Sammy just hosed it off every so often, and when he did it smelled wonderful, a mixture of dust and wet stone.

Outside there was a hose for washing and showers, a Weber grill for summer cooking, and an outhouse in the back.

Lucky heard a radio announcer's smooth radio voice plus Sammy's growly one as she followed HMS Beagle inside.

"Man, I tried melting it. Wouldn't melt. Tried grating it. Turns into dough. It must be some kind of secret weapon," Short

Sammy was saying. In the center of the room, at a rough wooden table that had once been a spool for coiling electrical wire, Lincoln leaned over a small bag of Fritos, eating out of it with a spoon. Nearby on the table was a length of cord with knots in it.

"Sammy's been experimenting with the Government Surplus cheese," Lincoln explained to Lucky. The radio announcer was telling about traffic tie-ups.

"So far, nobody can figure out what to do with it to make it something you'd want to *eat*," Sammy said. He pushed back the brim of his cowboy hat and frowned at the cheese. "The chili's

good, though. Made it with U.S. Government Surplus canned pork. Help yourself."

Quite a lot of people, especially Brigitte, had a strong opinion that Short Sammy used too much grease in his cooking. Brigitte insisted that Lucky should very politely say she wasn't hungry if he offered her anything to eat.

"Okay, yes, please," she said. Sammy opened another snack-size bag of Fritos and gave it to Lucky with a tin spoon.

"Pan's outside. Lid's hot."

Lucky lifted the lid with a rag, set it on a rock, and spooned beans and pork into the small bag of Fritos. She replaced the lid.

". . . a fender bender," said the radio announcer, "on the 101 South into downtown L.A. Slow going on the 10 East due to an oil spill in the car-pool lane. Better take the 60 if you can. That three-car pileup on the Pasadena Freeway near the four level has been cleared. . . ."

Short Sammy poured hot water over coffee grounds in a sock filter and shook his head. "That L.A. traffic is terrible," he said, sounding pleased. The traffic report always cheered him up. "Today's Saturday, and it's as bad as Monday rush hour." He poured dark black coffee into a tin mug.

"So what happened with the snake?" Lincoln asked, digging out the last of his chili-and-Fritos and licking the spoon.

"I scared it away." Lucky plopped into a chair. "It was a red racer." Short Sammy's recipe was a perfect meal because it was extremely delicious, plus no dishes to wash except your spoon and the pan once it was empty.

Short Sammy turned off the radio even though the traffic report wasn't over. "Red racers are good people, man," he said. "They get rid of the rattlers and side-winders."

"I *know*," Lucky said. "But Brigitte hates them. This chili is good."

Sammy waved at flies with his mug. Then he said a strange thing. "Brigitte's all right. She just needs something to do. She's bored."

Lucky's opinion was that Brigitte's job of being her Guardian was totally already something to do. How could she be bored with that? Plus, except for Lucky's own work at the Found Object Wind Chime Museum and Visitor Center, the Captain's mail-sorting job, and Dot's Baubles 'n' Beauty Salon, there were no jobs in Hard Pan no matter how much you wanted one.

"Too bad she can't open a restaurant or something," said Lincoln, who loved Brigitte's French way of making an apple pie. "I bet people would come from Talc Town and all over, plus the caravans of geologists from L.A. and regular tourists." As Lucky watched, he picked up his cord from the table, then pulled the two ends apart and a whole row of knots came magically undone. Right away he started tying new ones.

Lucky imagined a restaurant where the menu had things like tongue and sweetbreads, which are really some kind of *glands*, and oysters and snails and rabbits—things she was pretty sure French people sat around eating morning, noon, and night. She doubted there would be any customers for a restaurant like that in Hard Pan.

Short Sammy squatted by HMS Beagle, scratching her behind the ears. HMS Beagle loved Short Sammy's house because the rock floor was very cool to lie on, and because Short Sammy was her best friend after Lucky, ever since he pulled fifteen cactus spines out of her muzzle with his pliers when she was a puppy. "I wonder what they make that cheese *out* of," Sammy said.

Suddenly Lucky got a picture in her mind of the magazines Brigitte's mother sent from France, with pictures of beautiful castles and houses. "Sammy," she said, "have you ever been to France?"

"Sure," said Short Sammy, "but that was a lifetime ago."

Lucky knew he meant before he hit rock bottom, back when he still drank rum and homemade wine.

"There's a very famous museum in France," Lincoln said.

"Yeah, the Louvre. I remember a café near there," said Short Sammy.

"So would you rather live in France or Hard Pan?"

Short Sammy gave HMS Beagle a final scratch on her belly and squinted up at Lucky from under the brim of his cowboy hat. He stood, knees popping like when you pop your knuckles, and pivoted on the heel of his pointy-toed boot. "Look, man," he said, and went to a window, which was a large square cut out of the tin wall at exactly the right level to make a frame for Lucky's face. Short Sammy and Lucky were the same height, except the boots and hat gave him some extra. "Look at that," he said.

Lucky looked out at the jumble of trailers, sheds, outhouses, shacks, and rusty vehicles below. Dot was in her backyard hanging small white towels on a clothesline. At the edge of town Lucky's canned-ham bedroom trailer curled in a half circle with the other trailers it was connected to. "What?" she said, looking for the thing Short Sammy wanted her to see.

Lincoln came to the open doorway to look out in the same direction.

"Just Hard Pan," Short Sammy said. "HP, pop. 43. And everything that *isn't* Hard Pan. Look." Lucky did.

Past the town the desert rolled out and out like a pale

green ocean, as far as you could see, to the Coso foothills, then behind them, the huge black Coso Range like the broken edge of a giant cup that held tiny Hard Pan at its bottom. The sky arched up forever, nothing but a sheet of blue, hiding zillions of stars and planets and galaxies that were up there all the time, even when you couldn't see them. It was kind of peaceful and so gigantic it made your brain feel rested. It made you feel like you could become anything you wanted, like you were filled up with nothing but hope.

HP, she was thinking. HP stood for Hard Pan, but, she realized, it could also stand for Higher Power. Maybe Hard Pan was Short Sammy's Higher Power because of its slowness and peacefulness and sweet-smellingness, even though it was old and junky and out in the middle of nowhere. Lucky wondered if she could ever get Brigitte to love Hard Pan as much as she loved France.

Sammy's corrugated roof made tiny pinging sounds, almost like raindrops, as it expanded in the sun.

"The museum I meant," said Lincoln, "is, I don't know how you pronounce it, Le Musée Mondial du Nœud. It's a knot museum. I found out about it in *Knot News*."

Lucky sighed. Her brain was clogged up with questions, and she didn't even know exactly what they were.

Short Sammy had gone back to frown at the block of cheese on his table. "The only thing left, man, is to fry this thing in bacon grease," he said.

10. the urn

On Sunday morning Lucky woke up wanting to ask Lincoln something important. She phoned him, and they decided to meet right after breakfast up at the post office, since it was closed and nobody would be around.

Lucky wanted to talk to Lincoln about an urn she had. Not everyone who dies gets buried in the ground. Some people are cremated, which Lucky had not known about until her mother died. She found out that being cremated is where they take the dead person to a place called a crematory and put them in a box like a casket. The box goes through a special process—Short Sammy explained this—and afterward all that is left are little particles and ashes.

Then they put the particles and ashes into something called an urn.

If you never saw an urn before you would probably think it was a shiny metal vase for flowers, except it has a hinged lid with a latch to keep it solidly closed so nothing can spill out if it gets accidentally knocked over.

Two days after Brigitte had arrived in Hard Pan with her little suitcase, a strange man in sunglasses and a suit came and gave the urn to Lucky. She had thought that was a mistake, because she was only eight at the time and didn't know what she was supposed to do with it. So she tried to give it back.

The strange man had said to her, "These are your mother's remains. There will be a memorial service where you can fling them to the wind."

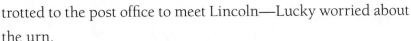

Lucky had stared at the man. She did not understand what he was talking about.

That was two years ago. But still now, every so often—and today was one of those times, while she and HMS Beagle trotted to the post office to meet Lincoln—Lucky worried about the urn.

Seen from a little distance, Lincoln looked better, in Lucky's opinion—you could imagine how he'd look when he grew into his ears. Like, as he got older his head wouldn't look as big and his neck would definitely look less scrawny. So far he didn't look like a president, which was what his mother was hoping and which was why she named him Lincoln Clinton Carter Kennedy. Lucky knew he'd rather be president of the International Guild of Knot Tyers. Mothers have their good sides, their bad sides, and their wacky sides, but Lucky figured Lincoln's mother had no way of knowing at the time he was born that he would turn out to be so dedicated about knots.

"Lincoln," Lucky said, squatting down to look at the lines

he'd drawn in the dirt, "do you remember when my mother died?"

"I don't remember *her* very well, but I do remember the . . . what do you call it. Not the funeral but the—"

"Memorial."

"Yeah. Don't you remember it?" Lincoln scratched HMS Beagle's soft chest.

"Kind of." It was almost *exactly* two years ago. Lucky did remember most of it strongly, but she wanted to know what Lincoln would say. "What do you remember about it?"

Lincoln squinted at her and went back to his sand drawing, which turned out to be some kind of hitch. Even when Lincoln glanced at something for only a tiny second, it was a

piercing and thorough glance, like with X-ray eyes. "Everyone in the whole town went," he said. "All the cars and trucks in a slow line, some dogs following along. It was at the old abandoned dugouts, on the open desert outside town, so there wasn't any shade. But the sun was going down and it was cooling off and people stood around and Short Sammy played the guitar. He played 'Amazing Grace' and everybody sang along and it was really sad and beautiful." Lincoln frowned at the ground. "I remember how, especially out overlooking the whole desert, there was that special smell from after it—" Lincoln's cheeks and the tips of his ears suddenly got red.

Lucky finished what Lincoln was going to say. "After it rains. I know, okay? That smell reminds me, too. You don't have to completely never mention rain. It wasn't like it was the *rain's* fault that it happened."

"Okay," he said, gouging his lines in the sand more deeply.

"I was supposed to spread her ashes in the wind," Lucky said. "Because I was the next of kin."

"Why didn't you?"

Lucky didn't answer right away. She was remembering that during a secret time in her bedroom, just before the memorial, she had opened the urn to look inside. The particles were like different sizes of whitish sand. But when she looked closely she could tell that they were little pieces of bone.

Lucky's hand fit inside the opening at the top of the urn. She had reached in. She was scared and excited, as if doing this was both right and wrong at the same time. Her fingers felt some dry, feathery stuff, and a lot of light, brittle bits.

They were the remains. The remains of her mother. She had very carefully closed and latched the lid of the urn and put it on her bed. She lay down on her side and curled herself around it.

At first she lay with one hand touching the urn. But after a while she put her arms all the way around it, like a child hugs a doll or a mother holds a child. Then she sat up and opened the lid again and let some of her tears fall inside. She wanted to mix her tears with the remains of her mother. She didn't know if this was allowed, so she did it very privately and quietly without telling anyone.

"Because they were the *remains* of my *mother*," Lucky finally explained.

Lincoln nodded. "People kept trying to get you to pop the cork off that vase," he said, "and they kept saying there was such a nice gentle breeze to carry the ashes out into the desert. Everyone wanted to convince you—"

"Urn," said Lucky. "It's called an urn. There was a little group of burros watching us." There were four of them, standing in profile on the crest of one of the hills by the dugouts, looking down at the people from the sides of their faces.

Up until then, Lucky hadn't known about scattering the ashes of a person who died. Someone had explained that people like to give the ashes back to the earth, that it was a way for her mother to become part of the desert and always be near Lucky.

But that made no sense. If you fling something away, like the remains of your own mother, if you throw those remains out into the desert, how does that make her near to you? Lucky had clutched the urn to her chest and stared at the burros and tried to know what to do.

Lucky remembered Brigitte's hand on her shoulder, the type of firm grip you would have if you were trying to keep a puppy from running away. She'd said it was time to go back, and that Lucky could bring the urn and she could keep it. But then all of a sudden Lucky didn't want it. She shoved it at Brigitte, as if it were only a vase for flowers after all, and ran to sit on Dot's tailgate so she could ride home backward, watching the burros on the hill until she couldn't see them anymore.

"It was your father," said Lincoln, "who made everyone leave you alone. He said the decision was yours, and whatever it was it would be the right one."

"My *father*? My father wasn't even *there*! I've never even *met* him!"

Lincoln's ears turned red again. "Don't you remember the tall guy with sunglasses? He was the only one wearing a suit in the heat."

"That was the *crematory* man," said Lucky, but she could feel something squeezing her heart in her chest. "What do you mean, my *father*?"

"I just remember people saying he was Brigitte's former husband, from before, and I thought that was weird," said Lincoln. "But then Dot was telling people, 'Lucky's father made all the arrangements,' and pointing to him with her chin like she does." He stood up and took a few steps back, like he was afraid of what Lucky would do.

Lucky smeared the knot design with the heel of her sneaker. "That whole deal is so *stupid*," she said. "If he was my *father*, why didn't he say so?"

"Listen," said Lincoln. "Here." He pulled a knot out of his pocket. It was large and complicated looking, made from blue and green silky cords. "It's called the Ten-Strand Round knot."

It looked like a piece of jewelry, intricate and beautiful.

For some reason, this made tears surge into Lucky's eyes, which was very embarrassing. "Lincoln," she said. "People think you're kind of clueless, but you're really not."

"I know I'm . . ." Lincoln used his stick to write the last word in the dirt road: K-N-O-T.

Then he showed the stick to HMS Beagle and threw it with a graceful long overhand toss and she ran and caught it in her mouth by leaping into the air, and brought it back to him so he could do it again.

Lucky cupped Lincoln's gift in her hand. The neat round buttonlike knot had no cord ends sticking out that might unwind, and you could never in a million years decipher how Lincoln had made it. You'd never find out how he had taken cords that were pretty useless, just lying around in someone's drawer, and looped and threaded them over and over in a special way until they ended up becoming a beautiful knot.

Never before had Lucky realized that Lincoln's knot-tying brain secretions gave him such a special way of seeing. She had thought he tied knots for practical reasons, in case there was ever a boat that needed to be tied to a dock, or a swing to be hung from a tree. Now she knew that Lincoln was really an artist, who could see the heart of a knot.

Lucky wished she were an artist too, and could organize all

the complicated strands of her life—the urn she still had, the strange crematory man, Brigitte and Miles, HMS Beagle and Short Sammy, the Captain and the anonymous people and Dot and even Lincoln himself, and weave them into a beautiful neat ten-strand knot.

11. smokers anonymous

Lucky had had the day off on Saturday because there was no twelve-step meeting that day. So on Sunday afternoon, she picked up cigarette butts and other trash left over from Friday's Alcoholics Anonymous meeting. She collected plenty of butts, because the ex-drinkers stood around talking and smoking before their meeting. The ashtrays were big coffee cans and flowerpots filled with sand—and they were always loaded with butts that the ex-smokers didn't want to see or smell before *their* meeting.

Lucky went around back to the Dumpster and stored her broom and rake against it. She heard someone moving chairs inside the museum, so she eased herself quietly into her lawn chair to listen.

The best part of the meetings came after they were done reading from a book called *Twelve Steps and Twelve Traditions*. Even though that part was a little bit boring, Lucky listened carefully for information about how to find your Higher Power. Then came the part where people told their most interesting and horrifying stories of how they hit rock bottom.

First it was the Captain's turn. Before he got the part-time mail-sorting job at the post office, he was an airline pilot who had the calm, in-charge voice of a TV airline pilot, so Lucky recognized it easily. He said how he was addicted so bad to cigarettes that he even smoked in the shower. He smoked from the first moment he opened his eyes in the morning until he fell asleep at night. He smoked while he ate. He even burned a big hole in his bride's wedding dress the day they got married.

The story was excellent so far. Then the Captain told about how his wife gave him a choice: quit smoking or she would divorce him.

"I told her, how about I switch to low tar, filtered," said the Captain. "I thought it was a pretty big sacrifice for a Camel smoker. She didn't agree and she walked out. That was almost rock bottom. I remember thinking, 'My wife just left me! I can't quit smoking *now*!'"

People laughed and clapped.

The Captain went on. "But then I came to a meeting and started working the twelve steps. I found my Higher Power. And here I am."

Lucky's enzymes started churning. She leaned forward to listen carefully. Maybe the Captain would explain exactly *how* he found his Higher Power and also *where*, which would be extremely . helpful. So far, Lucky hadn't found a trace of *her* Higher Power, though she tried hard to be alert for the slightest hint of it.

Having a Higher Power could help a person know what to do about the problem of a Guardian who, every time it got too hot, or there was French music or a snake in the dryer, seemed like she might quit and go back home to France.

Someone cleared her throat and shouted, "I'm Mildred. I choose not to smoke."

Lucky almost tipped over in her chair. It was Mrs. Prender, Miles's grandma. Lucky had never heard her talk at any of the meetings.

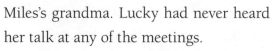

Mrs. Prender went on, "I was in the hospital with quadruple pneumonia. After the doc told me I'd die if I didn't quit smoking, I snuck out the back and lit a cigarette. I coughed so hard I broke a rib, so I had to quit for a while until they let me go home. Next day I dropped a cigarette on the couch and set it on fire, and then I set my *hair* on fire. I called the fire department and went outside to wait. Well, it was raining, so I stood there in the road bawling and trying to smoke a sopping-wet cigarette. But that wasn't rock bottom."

Mrs. Prender's story, Lucky decided, was even better than the Captain's.

"It was my grown daughter. I knew she'd been sneaking cigarettes since she was a girl, but I never done nothing about it. Figured, what could I say, a smoker myself. Couple years ago I get a call from the police in L.A., can I come pick up her little boy. She's been arrested for selling dope."

Lucky frowned. The little boy had to be Miles. But Miles's

mother was supposed to be in Florida, nursing her sick friend.

Mrs. Prender went on. "I go on down to L.A. for my grandson. My daughter gets a long jail sentence. So I figure—this is it. I'm not bringing up *another* kid with myself setting a bad example." Mrs. Prender blew her nose loudly. "Once I decided to quit, it was like turning off a light switch. I just did it. That was almost two years ago."

Lucky had the same jolting feeling as when you're in a big hurry to pee and you pull down your pants fast and back up to the toilet without looking—but some man or boy before you has forgotten to put the seat down. So your bottom, which is expecting the usual nicely shaped plastic toilet seat, instead lands shocked on the thin rim of the toilet bowl, which is quite a lot *colder* and *lower.* Your bottom gets a panic of bad surprise. That was the same thump-on-the-heart shock Lucky got finding out that Miles's mother was in jail.

73

12. parsley

After dinner, Lucky stood at the sink washing the dishes. She was still thinking a little bit about Mrs. Prender, but mostly about parsley. Before Brigitte came to Hard Pan, Lucky had never imagined that parsley could be so important. Usually if she even noticed it, it was because of being in a fancy place like Smithy's Family Restaurant in Sierra City, where a hamburger came on a plate with a frizz of parsley for decoration.

You noticed Smithy's fanciness right away because of how the waitress, Lulu, neatly rolled up everyone's fork-knife-spoon set in its paper napkin, like a little present. This made you feel especially welcomed. Another excellent quality of Smithy's was that, if you asked her, Lulu would bring two extra lemon wedges for your fish sticks *at no extra charge*, on a tiny plate especially made for that type of delicacy. Some people's tiny plates had olives speared by toothpicks with cellophane ruffles. Or the sprig of parsley with your burger, which Smithy's Family Restaurant probably realized wasn't *necessary*, the way ketchup was, but which gave a certain elegance. Lucky noticed that most people in Smithy's didn't actually *eat* their parsley—it was there just for the fanciness of making a pretty green decoration and also because it looked healthy and made health-conscious people not worry so much about the bad cholesterol teeming around in their juicy hamburger.

To Brigitte parsley was *essential*, but not in the same way as at Smithy's. She chopped it into tiny bits and sprinkled it over practically everything, including food that regular people don't even realize *goes* with parsley. She fanned it over cucumbers, noodle soup, beans, and garlic toast. She added it to gravy, eggs, melted butter dip, and especially to free Government food. And deep down Lucky had to admit that it gave everything a cleanness and an herb-ness, without being show-offish or making you think, *Oh, parsley again.*

Since Brigitte was so crazy about parsley, Lucky should not have been surprised that in France there is a special little hand grinder for it, where you stuff the parsley into a funnel and turn a handle and presto, perfect tiny fresh flakes come out underneath. You didn't need a knife or cutting board or anything—you could just go right up to the dish and turn the handle—no fuss, no muss. Of course, Brigitte's old mother had sent her a parsley grinder right off the bat when Brigitte told her how much she missed having one. And Brigitte had cried and acted like it was the best present she ever got in the world.

It was the parsley grinder's fault that Lucky hit rock bottom on Sunday after she came home from the Smokers Anonymous meeting. Brigitte made melted-cheese-and-sliced-tomato open-faced sandwiches with flecks of parsley on top for dinner. Lucky ate only half of hers because she wasn't too hungry, and she let Brigitte think this was because of the heat, instead of because of Short Sammy's Fritos-and-chili. But Lucky did have room for a piece of *clafouti*, which is a pancake-ish type of pie with fruit in it—this one had Government Surplus canned apricots, but you couldn't tell they weren't regular canned apricots.

It was the parsley grinder's fault, because the only thing Lucky did was to clean it in her usual thorough way after dinner. While she was at the sink, Miles came by—making screeching tire sounds—to forage for cookies. Brigitte ruffled his hair and said he could have a piece of *clafouti*. As she washed the grinder, Lucky bent one of the little spokes a teeny bit. She did it completely one hundred percent by accident and didn't even realize.

But when she put the two clean parts together, snapping the spokes back into the funnel, she discovered that the handle wouldn't turn.

She showed Brigitte.

Brigitte said, *"Oh, la vache,"* which means, as Lucky had learned, "Oh, the cow." But she said it the way you would say, "Oh, what a pain," or "Oh, good grief." It was never really about cows whatsoever when Brigitte said, *"Oh, la vache."*

Brigitte tried to bend the spoke back to its normal position. She made a *pfff* sound of being frustrated.

Miles swallowed a mouthful of *clafouti* and said, "You should get Dot to fix that parsley thing. She has lots of pliers and little jewelry tools."

"Wait a sec," Lucky said. "Let me try first." She got a table knife and very carefully wedged the spoke back in place. But she bent the next spoke in another wrong direction.

Brigitte sighed and went to the phone. "'Allo, Dot?" she said when she'd dialed. You mostly didn't need a phone book in Hard Pan because everybody's phone number began with the same first three numbers, so you only had to remember the other four. Dot's were 9876—easy. "Can we come over with a little thing to fix? We need to borrow those pliers with the tiny end."

Lucky and Miles watched Brigitte talk. She used one hand to hold the phone and the other to show the tapering ends of the pliers, even though Dot couldn't see her doing it. "You are not too busy?" Brigitte said to Dot. "Okay, yes, right now." She hung up.

"Lucky, I am going to wrap some *clafouti* to take to Dot. Can you look for the keys of the Jeep—I think on my desk. Miles, we drop you home on the way." As Lucky went to Brigitte's bedroom trailer, Miles began making screeching tire noises again.

The keys were not on the table. Lucky looked all around the room. "I can't find them," she called to Brigitte.

"Look in the drawer," Brigitte called back.

Lucky opened the drawer. Scissors, a tape measure, stamps, pencils, rubber bands. No keys. She closed the drawer and noticed Brigitte's little suitcase on a chair beside the table. It was closed, but the lid wasn't zipped.

"Never mind, Lucky!" Brigitte shouted. "I find them in here!"

Lucky had a bad feeling about that suitcase, which had *always* been stored at the back of Brigitte's closet.

"Lucky, are you coming to Dot's?"

Lucky stared at the suitcase. "No," she called, backing away from it. She went to the kitchen doorway. "I'll stay here and . . . work more on my ant report."

"You should anyway get ready for bed," Brigitte said. "School tomorrow. I come back soon."

Miles tire-screeched all the way to the Jeep.

78   Lucky went straight back to the suitcase. It was a bit bigger and deeper than a laptop carrier. Brigitte had come all the way from France with that one small case, thinking she was staying only a short time—until Lucky could be placed in a foster home. Probably she brought just a change of clothes. Now she had plenty of cotton surgical outfits from the thrift shop, which Lucky knew she liked because they were loose-fitting and cool, and because Brigitte said they made her feel Californian. Plus she had the Jeep and the three trailers and the computer that Lucky's father had given her. Plus she had Lucky.

This was the first time Lucky had seen the suitcase in two years.

Lucky lifted the lid. There were no clothes in it. Only a

stack of papers, and, on top, something very precious that was usually kept in a safe-deposit box at the bank in Sierra City.

Brigitte's passport.

Lucky didn't touch it or look at the other papers. Usually she would have examined them all very thoroughly. But the passport was enough. The only reason people need a passport is when they travel from one country to another country. Now she realized what was going on.

Lucky trudged back to the kitchen trailer. She suddenly understood that she'd been doing everything backward. She'd thought you looked for your Higher Power and when you found it you got special knowledge—special *insight*—about how the world works, and why people die, and how to keep bad things from happening.

But now she knew that wasn't the right order of things. Over and over at the anonymous meetings she'd heard people tell how their situation had gotten worse and worse and worse until they'd hit rock bottom. Only after they'd hit rock bottom did they get control of their lives. And *then* they found their Higher Power.

Another part of finding your Higher Power was to do a fearless and searching moral inventory of yourself. But Lucky was too *mad* for a fearless and searching moral inventory. She was too *hopeless*. She'd do it later. Right now she had proof that Brigitte was going back to France.

That put Lucky at rock bottom.

The anonymous people struggled with the next step after rock bottom, the getting-control-of-your-life step. Lucky pounded the Formica table with both fists, which made HMS Beagle leap to her feet and look at Lucky worriedly. It's almost *impossible* to get control of your life when you're only ten. It's other people, adults, who have control of your life, because they can abandon you.

They can die, like Lucky's mother.

They can decide they don't even *want* you, like Lucky's father.

And they can return to France as suddenly and easily as they left it, like Brigitte. And even if you carry a survival kit around with you at all times, it won't guarantee you'll survive. No kit in the world can protect you from all the possible bad things.

"But don't give up hope," Lucky said to HMS Beagle in a calming voice, because she didn't want her dog to worry. HMS Beagle looked a little reassured and she sat, but she still watched Lucky to see what was going to happen.

"I have an idea," Lucky told her slowly, thinking her thoughts from the bottom of her deep, rock-bottom pit. "I have an idea of something we can do to take control of our lives. It's kind of scary. We can run away." Lucky peered intently at HMS Beagle to see if she was willing.

HMS Beagle was.

Because Brigitte and her mother were always sending each other *bisous*, which means kisses, when they talked on the phone, Lucky figured that French people kiss more than regular people.

One thing Brigitte always did before Lucky went to bed was she came into Lucky's canned-ham trailer and sat on the narrow bed along the wall, and Lucky sat on her lap the same way you would sit on a chair. Brigitte hugged her strongly from behind and put her cheek against Lucky's cheek, and when she talked her chin poked Lucky's shoulder.

Even though it was babyish to sit on anyone's lap, Lucky was okay with being wrapped privately in Brigitte's arms. She liked having her face beside Brigitte's and smelling the clean-hair smell of her. At those times, she knew there were parts to the job of Guardian that Brigitte liked a lot, and hugging Lucky was one of them, and that made Lucky's heart fill up with molecules of hope and pump them all through her veins.

So that night, after Brigitte came home with her good-as-new parsley grinder, Lucky brushed her teeth, put on her short summer nightie, and waited. But Brigitte did not come. Lucky went into the kitchen trailer.

Brigitte sat cross-legged at the Formica table, one hand under her chin, the other clicking the mouse. A booklet was propped up next to the laptop. Lucky stuck her head into the tiny freezer, which contained two miniature ice cube trays, a Tupperware bowl full of more ice cubes, and a small plate of frozen grapes. She said, "I'm ready for bed now."

Without turning her head, Brigitte said, "Lucky, please close the door of the freezer. I am following my lesson."

"What lesson?" asked Lucky, thinking how odd it was to study after you finished school. Her report on The Life Cycle of the Ant was finished and ready to be turned in tomorrow, although the glued ants on the last page would not get a smiley face from Ms. McBeam for neatness. She grabbed an ice cube from the Tupperware bowl, took a deep breath of cold air, and closed the freezer.

"Lucky, *ma puce*," said Brigitte, peering at the screen, then at the booklet. "You must allow me to finish this without an interruption."

"Why do you call me your flea, anyway?" Lucky said, rubbing the ice cube over her forehead and cheeks. "Is it because I bite you and suck your blood, or what?"

"*Oh, la-la, la-LA, la-LA, la-LA!*" When Brigitte was a little bit upset, like the time Lucky accidentally squeezed most of the French mustard out of the tube, she clicked her tongue and said,

"*Oh, la-la.*" When she was frustrated, like the time Lucky spilled dry Jell-O on the floor and a trillion ants came inside during the night, Brigitte said, "*Oh, la-la, la-LA, la-LA!*" And when she was pretty mad, like when the monthly check came late, Brigitte said, "*Oh, la-la, la-LA, la-LA, la-LA!*"

Lucky continued, even though the four *la-LA*s made her nervous. "Is it because I bother you and make you itch? Do I give you bumps on your skin?" Rubbing the back of her neck with ice, Lucky moved toward Brigitte.

Brigitte slammed closed the lid of her computer with one hand and stood up, blocking Lucky's view of the booklet. "Lucky, I cannot think when you talk so much *bêtises* . . . silly stuff." Brigitte yanked a ragged wire-mesh fly-swatter from a peg and slapped it hard against the table edge. A fly took off from the spot and circled overhead.

Brigitte tried to swat it in flight. "That stupid fly," she said. "She always escapes!" She clapped the swatter back on its wall hook.

Thinking that a real mother would never be so mean and that a real mother would share all her secrets, especially the secret of her mysterious lessons and the secret of her passport, Lucky took the flyswatter, waited until the fly landed, tapped it lightly, and scooped it up, fluttering. She opened the screen door and shook the fly off into the hot night.

Hooking the swatter back on its peg, Lucky said in a dignified voice, "I'm going to bed now. And by the way, a fly is 'it,' not 'she.'"

"*Pfff,*" said Brigitte, and shrugged, turning back to her laptop. "Lucky, I cannot stop following this lesson right now. Go to bed. I check you later. *Bisous.*"

"*Pfff,*" said Lucky, and got a look at the booklet over Brigitte's shoulder. The top part was in French, so Lucky skipped down, where underneath were the words:

Certified Course in Restaurant Management and Administration with Diploma from the Culinary Institute of France in Paris

That was how Lucky learned for sure why Brigitte was planning to return home. She was getting an online diploma from some French school in running a restaurant. This explained all those times Brigitte talked about how much she wished she had a job. All along Brigitte had been telling Lucky that what she really wanted was to go back to France and run a restaurant.

Lucky sat on her bed thinking this over. Some tears came out of her eyes, and she wished Brigitte would come—not so she could sit on her lap and let herself be hugged, but so that Brigitte could see what a sad and abandoned child she was, an orphan whose Guardian was too busy for hugging. As soon as she began imagining the shocked and concerned look on Brigitte's face if Brigitte were to see her crying, Lucky cried some more. HMS Beagle, who slept on the round rug beside the bed, came to lay her head on Lucky's pillow.

"Poor, poor HMS Beagle," Lucky whispered. "When Brigitte goes back to France you will have to go live with Short Sammy, or with Miles and his grandma. I doubt the orphanage in L.A. will admit dogs."

Sadly, lonesomely, she got into her hot bed, kicking the sheet away.

Lucky lay on her back, her pillow feeling as hot as if it had been baked in the oven. She decided to run away very soon. If she ran away, Brigitte would have to call the police, and the police would call her father and tell him he had better have a talk with Brigitte about doing her Guardian job a little better than *that*. Lucky liked the idea that by running away she could make people do things they wouldn't do otherwise.

Brigitte was entirely wrong as a choice for a Guardian, Lucky decided. Even though she had come to California right after Lucky's mom died to take care of Lucky, she was just too French and too unmotherly. She should have had lessons or some kind of manual on how to do the job. If they had online courses in how to manage restaurants, they should at least have courses on how to be a good Guardian or even how to be a good actual birth mom, which was a more important job than restauranting. Lucky thought that writing this manual would be a good project for her once she was grown up.

The manual would be called,

Certificated Course in How to Raise a Girl
for Guardians and Actual Mothers
with Diploma

When she ran away, everyone would be worried and sad, and Miles would miss her horribly. The thought of how much Miles would miss her made Lucky cry again. And Lincoln! Probably Lincoln would be so sad his brain would quit sending knot-tying secretions. Tears ran down the sides of her face and into her ears, which felt strange. She needed to blow her nose but sniffed hard instead. The mucus she swallowed tasted like the biggest sadness in the world. Even the crickets outside sounded mournful.

Drying her face with the sheet, Lucky turned on her side and flipped the soggy pillow over. Running away takes very good planning. She already had her survival kit. She thought of a few more items to take that most people wouldn't consider necessary for survival. They were not things you can eat or drink or use for protection or to get rescued or to keep from being bored. They were things that Lucky's heart needed in order to stay brave and not falter.

She would run away to the old miners' dugout caves and stay about a week, then she would see what next. If the rescuers and the police still hadn't found her, maybe she would sneak back into the town on a Saturday morning and hide under the porch of Dot's Baubles 'n' Beauty Salon at the back of Dot's house to find out what people were saying about her disappearance while they got their hair done.

Lucky arranged some permed curls over her ear to keep bugs from crawling in, and she was almost asleep when she heard Brigitte tiptoe to her open doorway.

"Are you asleep, Lucky?" she whispered.

Lucky pretended to be sleeping. She'd given Brigitte a chance to talk, but Brigitte had had more important things to do. Now it was too late. Lucky breathed deeply and slowly, in and out, and waited for Brigitte to tiptoe away, but she must have stayed there in the doorway for a long time. Lucky had not heard the sound of her leaving when she finally did fall asleep for real.

14. the first sign

Lucky didn't realize that she would get Three Signs telling her that it was the exact perfect day to run away. Her running-away idea was even more definite Monday morning, and it was very thorough, rather than being just a whim where you could make mistakes or do something tragical. She had told HMS Beagle that they would probably take off as soon as she got home from school.

She had to jog uphill, her survival kit slapping her back, to meet the school bus in time. She saw Lincoln waiting in the very back of the bus and Miles skipping—he had just learned to skip—down from his house. At the wheel, her elbow sticking out the window, Sandi, the bus driver, glowered at Lucky. She looked at her watch and shook her head. The exhaust from the bus drowned out the fresh smell of the new morning.

"Hurry *up*, Miles," Lucky yelled as she waited by the front door of the bus, panting. "He's coming," she called up to Sandi, who shook her head again.

"We got fifty miles to cover before the bell rings," Sandi said, as she always did, "and I'm not waiting."

"He's only five," said Lucky.

Sandi flipped on her turn signal and checked the side view mirrors.

"Here he is," Lucky said, and grabbed Miles's plastic sack so he could climb up the two deep steps quickly.

"Don't help me, Lucky," he said. "I can climb up by myself."

"Let's *go*," said Sandi.

"Did you see me skip?" Miles asked Sandi. "I skipped all the way down the hill."

"Rear of the bus," said Sandi, who didn't want kids sitting close enough to talk to her.

Lucky followed Miles past sixty empty seats, to the last long bench, where Lincoln was knotting a piece of yellow twine.

"Did you see me skip?" Miles asked Lincoln.

"No," said Lincoln, frowning at his knot.

Lucky looked out the rear window. HMS Beagle stood watching the bus, then turned and trotted toward home. She would be waiting when the bus arrived back at four fifteen, as she did every day.

Miles sat by the window, took *Are You My Mother?* out of the plastic sack, and held it on his lap. He had an almost-healed scab on one knee and a new-looking scrape on the other. One sneaker had a hole in the side where his little toe poked through. The sun shining through the window glinted on his coppery hair, which was mashed down on one side.

The bus climbed up and out of the valley, then turned and joined the highway to Sierra City. Miles swiped the dusty window with his hand, wiped his hand on his pants, and pointed to the forest of Joshua trees. "Is this Short Sammy's adopted highway?" he asked.

"Not yet. Wait, here comes the little sign," Lucky said. Then it flashed by:

ADOPT-A-HIGHWAY
SAMMY DESOTO

Adopting a highway is not like adopting a child. Lucky planned to adopt seven or eight highways when she got old enough, if she had time. What it means is that you take care of this certain stretch of road by picking up all the litter every week. Also you get an official orange vest and hard hat, and special trash bags, *plus* you get a sign on the highway that people can admire as they drive past.

"Was that it? Sandi should stop so we can read it," Miles complained. "Some people need more time to sound out their words."

Lucky and Lincoln eye-smiled at each other without letting Miles see. That, thought Lucky, was the First Sign. The way she and Lincoln understood right then what each other was thinking.

"She can't stop or we'll be late for school," Lincoln said. "Check out how the highway along here is so clean, though. Short Sammy cleans it."

"In his orange vest?"

"Yeah."

Miles began making frog croaking noises. Lincoln immediately put on his headphones. He didn't have a player for them to plug into, but by wearing them Lucky figured he could concentrate better on his knots. Finally Lucky couldn't stand any more frog croaking, so she told Miles a story of how the Joshua trees were playing Statues, and when they thought you weren't looking they changed their weird positions.

"If you stare at them very quietly you'll see them move," she said. Miles rested his forehead on the dusty window and stared out for about three minutes. Then he said, "Lucky?"

"What."

"Do you have an extra Fig Newton?"

"Oh, Miles," she said, and dug a Fig Newton out of her tote bag. "Doesn't your grandmother ever comb your hair?"

"Sometimes," said Miles, lightly kicking the seat in front of him as he ate tiny bites of the cookie.

91

15. the second sign and the third sign

Lucky felt excited and impatient all day at school. Ms. McBeam read a thin book to the fifth grade about Charles Darwin, the scientist Lucky most admired. The totally amazing thing about Charles Darwin was how much he and Lucky were alike. For instance, in the book there was a part where Charles Darwin found two interesting beetles. To capture them, all he had was his hands, so he caught one in each hand. *Then*—and this was the great part—he found a third interesting beetle, so he popped it into his mouth! That was *exactly* something Lucky would do, except for the constant fact that *she* carried her survival backpack full of specimen boxes with her at all times.

Then Ms. McBeam showed pictures of polar bears in the snow and explained that Charles Darwin figured out that animals survive by adapting to their environment. Polar bears are white like the snow so they will be harder to see and they can sneak up on their next meal. (And also to make them harder to be spotted by other animals or people who hunt *them*.) The same with insects who look like the plants they eat—except they're hiding from the birds that want to eat them, Ms. McBeam explained.

At that exact moment, Lucky looked at her sandy-colored arms and realized, finally, why her hair and eyes and skin were all one color! Charles Darwin had a very good point. She was like those lizards and sidewinders—exactly the color of the sand outside. *She* blended in too.

She, Lucky, was perfectly adapted to her environment, the northern Mojave Desert, and she knew that the sameness of her coloring was exactly right. It was the Second Sign, as significant and thrilling as the secret eye-smiling First Sign on the bus.

Just after lunch, when Lucky thought she could not bear to wait until three fifteen for the school bus to arrive for the ride home, the principal came to Room Four. Lucky sat forward in her seat to stare at Ms. Baum-Izzart, who was eight months pregnant and wore black pants and a tight-fitting flowered shirt that showed exactly the shape of her pregnant stomach. Ms. Baum-Izzart smiled at Ms. McBeam and at the fifth graders. She put her two hands on her shirt, holding the sides of her stomach. Lucky noticed that there were slightly darker marks where Ms. Baum-Izzart put her hands, like the dark stains on the sides of Miles's pants where he wiped his hands. She figured Ms. Baum-Izzart spent a lot of time feeling the interesting huge round ball of her stomach.

A part of Lucky wished the principal would suddenly start having the baby so they could all watch. Maybe Lucky could even help in some very important way, like if they needed mineral oil and only she had some at the last minute.

Instead of going into labor, Ms. Baum-Izzart said, "There's a pretty big dust storm coming off the dry lake. We're sending the children from outlying areas home early. I want those of you who ride the school bus to take all your belongings and meet your bus outside right now. *Walk*, please; do not run."

The kids who lived in Sierra City groaned because they had to stay till the normal end of school. But for Lucky this was the Third Sign that of all possible days to run away, today was the exact right one.

". . . fifty-five-mile-per-hour winds in high-desert areas . . ." the tinny voice of the radio announcer was saying as Lucky climbed on the bus. ". . . trailers and campers should avoid Highway 395 in the passes due to high winds." Sandi jerked her head, to show Lucky that she should hurry up to the rear, which Lucky already knew from having Sandi as her bus driver since kindergarten.

Miles and Lincoln followed her down the aisle, past a few kids who got off at Talc Town, and Sandi started up. Usually Lucky worried about dust storms because all you could do was go inside and close all the windows, no matter how hot it was. Dust came inside anyway, and when the storm was over, she and Brigitte had to vacuum and wipe down everything. Brigitte always said the devil left his back door open and let all the dust of hell blow into her kitchen.

But today Lucky *loved* the dust storm. She would be home early and have more time for running away before dark.

"Lucky," said Miles as he flung his plastic bag on the seat. "When is Ms. Baum-Izzart going to have her baby?"

"Pretty soon," said Lucky. "Maybe in about three weeks."

"Will the storm be over when she has it?"

Lucky clicked her tongue and rolled her eyes at him. "Of *course.*"

"What about Chesterfield's baby?"

"What about him?"

"Well, where will Chesterfield and her baby go during the dust storm?"

"Oh, probably to the dugouts, where they'll be nice and protected. They'll wait there till it's over," said Lucky.

"My grandmother said you could die in a dust storm," said Miles.

"But not Chesterfield or her child." Lucky peered out the window. The sky had turned brownish and seemed lower, like a giant dirty blanket drifting down to cover everything. It was growing dark because the thick dust blocked the sun. She turned back to Miles, who was looking up at her worriedly. "Burros help each other. They stand head to tail with another burro and each one's tail swishes the flies from the other's face. In a dust storm they all stay close together. Besides, they have long thick eyelashes to protect their eyes. Chesterfield is totally adapted to her desert habitat. Do you want me to explain about habitats?"

"No," said Miles, and opened *Are You My Mother?* He turned the pages slowly, reading it aloud from memory, his small dirty index finger more or less following the words.

Lincoln rolled his eyes at Lucky, which she considered Part B of the First Sign. She knew he meant that listening to Miles sound out *Are You My Mother?* again, after having heard him do it eight thousand times on the bus ride to school and back, was too boring to bear. He put his headphones on and got out a piece of rope.

Even though she was tempted to tell Lincoln about her decision to run away, the valve that kept secrets locked up in Lucky's heart was clamped shut. Lucky's heart would have liked to share her secret with Lincoln, but his knowing could wreck everything. So the heart-valve stayed closed, and Lucky kept her dangerous secret to herself.

16. getting ready to run away

Lucky's original plan had been to *pretend* to go to her job at the Found Object Wind Chime Museum and Visitor Center early, right after coming back from school, rather than her usual time of late afternoon. But instead she'd run away. Then when the bus arrived hours before the regular time and Lucky saw Brigitte's Jeep and Short Sammy's Cadillac parked at the Captain's house, she decided to leave right away. Brigitte wouldn't miss her for a long time. But first there were important supplies to get at home.

Even though the bus had come back way earlier than usual, HMS Beagle was waiting in the usual place. It was too windy for Lucky to explain about the Three Signs, and anyway, they had to watch out for things blowing around, like dead bushes and pieces of trash. Lucky knew that it could get so windy that even roofs blew off houses, and you couldn't tell what direction you were going because the sun was blotted out. Tiny twisters of sand rose up from the ground, as if miniature people were throwing handfuls in the air. A loose flap of tin banged on someone's roof, and the wind tugged the tamarisk trees sideways.

Lucky spread a towel on her bed next to her survival kit backpack. It was already ready, but she checked again to be sure. Crammed inside were:

- empty mint boxes for collecting specimens, scrounged from trash left by ex-smokers, plus a large tin for HMS Beagle's water bowl
- nail polish remover and cotton balls
- mineral oil for the glistening of eyebrows
- a survival blanket (kind of like very strong tin foil folded up into a tiny square)—not the keep-you-warm kind of blanket, but shiny so the rescue helicopter can spot it; also, if you know how, you can use such a blanket to collect drops of water to keep from dying of thirst. Lucky would figure out how this worked if the time came.
- *Twelve Steps and Twelve Traditions*, borrowed in order to study more about how to find your Higher Power
- pencil and notebook to describe specimens
- tiny packets of ketchup from McDonald's
- can of beans
- the Ten-Strand Round knot
- brand-new toothbrush from a teeth-cleaning at the Sierra City clinic, still in its original wrapper so that if she started to lose heart—"to lose heart"

being Lucky's favorite sad but exquisite phrase—she could get out a beautiful never-used toothbrush and make herself feel better

- half a tube of toothpaste
- bottle of water and bottle of Gatorade

The survival kit had everything she would need to keep from getting bored or too lonely, which are probably the worst dangers of running away.

On the towel she laid out her jacket and a roll of toilet paper. She wished she could take her pillow, but it was too bulky.

In the fridge she found two hard-boiled eggs, four carrots (HMS Beagle loved carrots), the Government Surplus cheese, which no matter how awful it was both she and HMS Beagle could eat in case they started starving to death, Fig Newtons, and a box of dry Jell-O (in a plastic Ziploc bag to ward off ants). HMS Beagle's kibble in another Ziploc bag.

Lucky looked around.

On the counter was Brigitte's metal parsley grinder, which Dot had fixed so it worked like new.

Lucky put it on the towel. Then suddenly she went back into the kitchen. She reached up and grabbed the urn with her mother's remains and her own dried-up tears inside. She added that to the pile and carefully rolled the towel up into a tight but bulky tube. She jammed it into a plastic grocery bag.

Lucky was ready to start running away when she realized

that she might never return to the half circle of trailers if the rescuers took her directly to the orphanage in Los Angeles. So she was about to go one last time into Brigitte's trailer, when she heard blasts of a tugboat coming closer and closer.

Oh, la-la, la-LA, la-LA, la-LA, she thought. *I'll never be able to run away with him here.*

"Go away, Miles," she yelled. "I'm busy!"

"Lucky, the storm is really bad! Everyone's at the Captain's house saying the power and the phones will probably go out. Can I come in?"

"No! Go away!"

"Why? I won't make noises!" Miles let himself in and took short skips to the Formica table. He pulled *Are You My Mother?* out of his Buy-Mor-Store sack. Its spine had been freshly mended with duct tape. "My grandma fixed my book," he said.

Lucky had no time to be nice. "That book is *wrecked*," she said. "It looks even worse now."

Miles smoothed the duct tape. "It's still fine inside," he said. "Could you read it to me?"

"Miles, get a life. You already know the story by heart, and it's boring."

"No, it's not! The part about the Snort is good, and so is the part where he finds his mother at the end."

"That bird is an idiot snotwad," said Lucky. "He doesn't even know"—Lucky took a breath—"he doesn't even realize *that his mother is in jail!*"

100

Miles sat still, looking down at his book. "She is not," he said in a small voice.

"Yes, she is! Your grandmother said so." Lucky leaned over Miles, her meanness gland pumping. "And *I'm* not your mother either! I'm not taking care of you! So go home!"

Miles looked up at her with his eyes full of tears. He threw the book on the floor and kicked it. He started crying hard. "I'm never coming back!" he shouted, and ran out into the wild brown wind.

Good, thought Lucky. Then for no reason she got a sudden exploding idea. She rushed to Brigitte's trailer and flung open the closet. The perfumy smell of Brigitte wafted out of it. There were jackets and a couple of dresses, and neatly folded piles of surgical pants and shirts. At the very end of the rod was Brigitte's red silk dress, in a clear plastic dry-cleaner's bag.

The dress felt like a pile of feathers, almost too light and silky to touch. It made Lucky feel she should wash her hands. It was a dress you would wear only for something very important, like coming to California to become someone's Guardian. The tag said "La Fortune, Galleries Lafayette, Paris." Brigitte hadn't worn it since the day she arrived, but Lucky still remembered the dancy twirly shimmeringness of that dress.

Lucky yanked off her jeans and top and left them on the floor. She pulled the silk dress over her head. The hem came to the tops of her socks. It was too loose to really fit her, but it felt different next to her skin, not at all like her regular clothes. It turned her into someone else, someone beautiful and sophisticated, who could make a dessert that had flames coming out of it on purpose. Her regular clothes were faded from many washings and from the sun, but the redness of this dress was the same thing for your eyes as a sonic boom is for your ears, or a jalapeño pepper is for your mouth.

She felt herself through the fabric and twisted like when you do the hootchy-kootchy, to move the silk against her skin. She felt sort of French and sort of lit-up and wished suddenly that Lincoln were there to see her. This was so strange to her, the flash-thought of Lincoln out of nowhere, that she made the thought go into a place inside that wasn't her brain, so she wouldn't have to think about it.

Lucky spread Brigitte's sunscreen on her hands, arms, face, and neck, carefully not getting much of it on the dress. Outside the wind was stronger, whooshing noisily. She rummaged through the kitchen tool carton until she found a dust mask that you used when you sanded the curved wood walls inside the trailers. She wasn't thinking in the same careful Running-Away-Project way as before, because now she had turned into a Brigitte-type of person.

The phone rang. It was Miles's grandmother, Mrs. Prender.

"Is Miles there?" she shouted. "I seen the school bus come back early."

"No," Lucky said.

"I want him home—the wind's getting bad. You seen him?"

"No," Lucky lied.

"Well, you do, make him stay put and call me so I can pick him up in the car."

"Okay, Mrs. Prender." She hung up.

Lucky considered swiping Brigitte's passport, because that was another way to stop her from leaving. But it wasn't the *best* way. The best way would be if Brigitte made her own *decision* to stay because she loved Lucky. And in order for Brigitte to realize how much she loved her ward, the ward had to run away. Then Brigitte would feel sorry and worried and abandoned, and that would make her understand exactly how Lucky felt.

The phone rang again. Lucky glared at it. She was way too busy for a zillion phone calls. This time it was Lincoln. She put one hand on her silk hip.

"Everyone's looking for Miles," he said.

"He's probably at Dot's or at the Found Object Wind Chime Museum and Visitor Center."

"You think—whoa!—our power just went out. Is yours on?"

"Yeah. Listen, I have to go."

"If you see Miles, tell him his grandma wants him."

Lucky held the receiver and felt Lincoln waiting at the other end. She realized she was probably talking to him for the last time, unless they allowed the orphans in the L.A. orphanage to make phone calls, which she doubted. Everyone was so worried about *Miles*, when it was *she* who would soon be gone forever.

"Lincoln," she said, and struggled around in her mind to figure out what she wanted to say. "You are . . . the best knot *artist* I ever met."

Lincoln was silent, either because he was too infected with shyness or because it was another Sign and he was guessing the truth. Very gently and sadly, she hung up.

17. hms beagle disobeys

A part of her mind was telling Lucky that if she ran away she would lose her job at the Found Object Wind Chime Museum and Visitor Center. That certain brain compartment also worried about getting in deep trouble and being sent away.

But a bossier, louder crevice of Lucky's brain argued that she had already *decided* about running away. There were already all of her *plans* and all the *supplies*, and all the hard *work* of running away. All that would be wasted if she gave up now.

Then *another* part of Lucky's brain reminded her that there was the new problem of Miles. She should be helping to find him. It was her fault that he was missing, even though, she reasoned, she'd *had* to get rid of him in order to run away herself. But this particular Running-Away was *her* Running-Away. If Miles had also run away, instead of just, for instance, hiding out under Dot's back porch, it would be like sharing it, and Lucky did not want to share it. If there was glory, she wanted all the glory. And if there were problems, well, they were his *mother's* problems, the price she paid for being in jail.

Lucky put her dust mask on to make herself quit thinking

and just *go*. She snatched up Miles's book and crammed it into the plastic sack with her rolled-up towel. Then she got her arms into her backpack straps, jumping to center it on her back. It weighed eight hundred pounds.

She soaked a dishtowel and draped it over her head, using Brigitte's sweatband to anchor it on top and safety-pinning it together under her chin. She looped the plastic sack over her wrist. Lucky and HMS Beagle ran down the trailer steps.

It was way, way noisier outside. The canvas awning strained and flapped as the wind roared; the trailers creaked and rocked on their blocks. The wind blew toward the open desert, which was where Lucky was heading, so at least she had it at her back.

With HMS Beagle trotting ahead, they crossed the invisible boundary of the edge of Hard Pan into the Bureau of Land Management land, leaving the town and walking onto the vast Mojave Desert. Lucky felt that it was good she was so well prepared—otherwise, she'd have been a tiny bit scared.

They struggled down the sandy road that led across the desert to some abandoned mines in the distant hills. Lucky knew it was important to stay on the rutted road to keep from getting lost. She kept a tight grip on her plastic sack, which twisted and strained to fly away. Her dishtowel flapped and made it hard to see, but was cool and kept some of the swirling sand out of her hair. Uprooted plants and old junk whipped past.

After about twenty minutes Lucky needed to pee. She went off to the side, watching for snakes and scorpions and nasty types of cactus, and squatted, pulling her underpants down and the silk dress up to her waist. She planted one shoe on the handles of the plastic sack to keep it from flapping away.

It was hard keeping her balance with the backpack on, but she didn't want to take the thing off and then have to put it on again with no chair or counter to back up to. She realized that the toilet paper was wrapped up in the towel inside the sack, and undoing everything to get it would be impossible. Right now for peeing it was okay—you just stayed squatting and the wind dried everything in a quick minute. But later on Lucky would need to organize her stuff better, with the toilet paper on top.

As she lurched to her feet and pulled her underpants up at the same time, the whole weight of the backpack seemed to shift and she lost her balance and fell backward. Stuff in her backpack crunched and something mashed into her spine. It made her feel discouraged, like if you took the word apart into two sections of *dis* and *couraged*. It was getting harder and harder to stay couraged.

She rolled over onto her hands and knees and stayed that way for a while, panting into her mask. Hard little rocks pressed against her knees through the silk and nipped her palms. Not a soul in the world knew where she was, or cared. She was nothing but a speck on the surface of the Earth. Lucky almost didn't have the strength to stand up again, but then HMS Beagle went bounding away down the road.

Even my dog abandons me, thought Lucky, but she heaved herself up, clutching the plastic bag, and plowed on.

Lucky stole her technique of keeping going from the anonymous twelve-step people, whose slogan is "One Day at a Time." If you think of undoing a big habit day after day for the entire rest of your life, you can't bear it because it's too overwhelming and hard, so you give up. But if you think only of getting through this one day, and don't worry about later, you can do it. Lucky used the "One Day at a Time" idea by putting one foot in front of the other without thinking about what would happen later. She knew she could do one step and then another step and then another step and then another step as long as she thought "One Step at a Time."

But the wind was a terribly strong enemy. Sometimes it pushed her so hard from behind that she thought it would knock her over. Once a huge thing that turned out to be most of a washing machine hurtled past her, and she saw a sheet and pillowcase—probably ripped by the wind from someone's clothesline—sailing out to the desert.

When HMS Beagle suddenly veered across the path to sniff at a pile of old rags, Lucky did not pause. She pressed on, believing the dugouts must be close now, though she couldn't see very far in any direction. The dugouts would give shelter from the wind. After a while, she looked back through the blast of dust. HMS Beagle was sitting by the rags.

"HMS Beagle, come!" she said, but her words were whooshed away by the wind. Lucky gestured with her whole arm for the dog to come. HMS Beagle sat.

Lucky grimly turned away and went on. Of course HMS Beagle was going to leave her all by herself! What worse thing could happen?

When the road curved around a low hill, Lucky suddenly couldn't get her bearings. Was this some fork she'd forgotten about? She didn't remember the road curving like that, which made her heart pump out waves of panic. The project was to run away, not to get *lost*. She looked behind her: nothing but the thick blanket of brown dust. But the hill on her right provided a buffer, so instead of turning back she pulled the dishcloth away from her face so she could peer around.

Halfway up the hill was a level shelf, and behind the shelf—the dugouts! Five uneven door-size holes leading to shallow caves in the hill. She'd gone much farther than she'd realized. Seeing the dugouts made Lucky feel almost like she'd come home.

Lucky staggered up to the first dugout, a cave about the size of her canned-ham trailer. In that protected spot, the roar and powerful force of the wind let go its grip, and Lucky shrugged off her backpack at last. At the cave entrance, she unrolled the towel and laid it out like a picnic blanket, weighting the corners with stones.

It was an excellent choice that she was wearing a beautiful silk French dress as her running-away outfit, although it was now covered with grit and dust. She arranged herself on the towel in a beauty-queen way. If Lincoln had been there, she would have asked him to teach her how to make a knot so strong it would never come undone.

Lucky rerolled the stuff from the towel into her jacket. She stripped off her mask and took a big swig of Gatorade. The dishcloth was completely dry now, and when she shook it out, she found her hair and ears, the corners of her eyes, her eyelashes and eyebrows were all full of sand.

She began to worry about HMS Beagle.

"HMS Beagle!" she shouted. "Beag!" She pictured her dog

meeting a sidewinder on the road. Or maybe she got conked by a flying lawn chair. What if HMS Beagle was in trouble? Why *else* wouldn't she have finally caught up?

Lucky was bone weary and couldn't bear the thought of going back into the windstorm, but she was also lonely and worried, and the worried part was strongest. Leaving the backpack, leaving the plastic bag, Lucky ran down the road to find her dog.

Heading *into* the wind turned out to be way, way harder, even without her backpack and supply sack. Lucky had to scuttle along doubled over, like an old woman, keeping her squinted eyes on the road. Without the mask or the dishcloth her face was completely exposed. She couldn't see more than a few feet ahead.

She almost tripped over HMS Beagle, who trotted up to her with her head low to the ground, her ears whipping forward. She touched Lucky with her nose and then abruptly turned and bounded back toward the town. Maybe HMS Beagle was right and they should go home. Lucky stopped.

"Hey, Beag!" she yelled. Then, faintly, she heard a cat or some other animal crying, and saw that HMS Beagle was nudging that pile of rags.

Very carefully Lucky approached the thing, which was huddled in a tight ball. It looked like the thing was rolled up in an old tablecloth or sheet. Sticking out of the roll was a small sneaker with a toe poking through a hole in the side.

18. cholla burr

Miles, she thought. *Oh, la vache.* She wanted nothing to do with him. She longed to turn around and go back to the dugout. Miles was way much too much trouble and he was ruining everything. He hadn't seen her, because he'd completely rolled himself up in the tablecloth, one he must have snagged as it flew by, so he'd never know she'd been there and neither would anyone else. She turned to go and the wind helped her, pushing her back to the shelter of the dugout. But when she was almost there she knew HMS Beagle was right. That dog would never have to do a searching and fearless moral inventory of *herself.* Lucky sighed and fought her way through the wind back to Miles.

He pressed his face, streaked with tears, snot, and dirt, into Lucky's front and gripped his arms around her neck. "I was waiting for Chesterfield to find me," he sobbed, "but a coyote came and snuffled me."

"That was only HMS Beagle," Lucky said. "The dugouts aren't far—let's go, quick."

"I can't. I have a cactus in my foot. It hurts!" Miles started crying again.

It was a cholla burr the size of a golf ball, a dozen of its needles stuck deep into Miles's heel. Lucky didn't touch it. She knew very well from the time *she* had stepped on one that you could *not* pull it out with your fingers. Plus she knew that it burned like fire underneath your skin.

"Where's your shoe?" she said into his ear. He hadn't loosened his grip on her neck.

"I don't know! I lost it."

"Okay, look. I'm going to carry you piggyback. You have to help by letting go and then climbing on me."

"Please don't trick me and leave me here, Lucky!"

"I promise I won't, Miles. Come on."

Even though she'd had a lot of practice lugging her survival kit backpack all the time, Lucky was surprised at how heavy a five-year-old boy could feel. She staggered back up the hill to the dugout, feeling as if the day had been going on for weeks.

Her worst thought was that she didn't have pliers to grip the cholla burr and pull it out. Even if she made a very clumsy glove by folding the dishcloth over and over on itself, the cholla's steel-hard needles would plunge right through the cloth and get stuck in her hand.

Miles sat on the towel with his bare foot propped on his other leg to keep anything from touching the burr and making it hurt worse. He gulped Gatorade, finishing the bottle. HMS Beagle spent a long time lapping water.

"I already tried to get it out," he said, "but it hurts your fingers to touch it."

"I know," Lucky said. She rummaged through her supplies and survival kit. She'd seen Short Sammy dislodge a burr stuck in a boot by slipping a fork between the needles and the leather and *flipping* it out, instead of trying to pull it out.

But Lucky didn't have a fork or even a comb, which also might have worked. She needed something *toothed*. But the toothbrush bristles were way too soft.

"Lucky?"

"Miles, I'm concentrating. What."

"Nothing."

Lucky sighed. "Okay, what?" she said in a nicer, paying-attention way.

"You don't look normal. You look kind of . . . fancy."

Lucky scowled.

"But you look pretty and kind of . . . grown up," he added.

Lucky thought of herself as someone highly adapted to her habitat, being all one colorless color, rather than pretty. She narrowed her eyes at Miles to see if he was up to something, but he was looking worriedly at the cholla burr, with its needle-sharp thorns sticking out in every direction—a dozen of them in his heel. She tucked the thought of prettiness into a safe crevice, for thinking about later.

Suddenly Miles said, "Is Brigitte coming to make our dinner?"

"No, Miles. We *ran away*."

"*I* didn't run away."

Lucky let that go.

"Then why is her thing for parsley here?" Miles asked.

"Just a keepsake, like when you want to remember someone and—" Lucky broke off. Her mind had found a great spectacular idea. She plucked Brigitte's gadget from the pile of supplies and released its little latch. The two parts separated—a funnel-like part where you crammed in the parsley and a little spoked part with a handle.

She gripped the top of Miles's foot in one hand. "Don't move," she said. Very carefully she angled the tin spokes under the cholla and with a hard, sure, sudden twist, she flipped the whole burr away.

"*Ow*," Miles cried.

All the needles were out. Lucky kicked the burr aside and then crushed it with a rock.

"This is quite a mild case," Lucky said professionally as she peered at the foot. "It will hurt for a while, so you have to be brave about that."

115

"I will," he snuffled. "I didn't run away on purpose, Lucky. I was just looking for Chesterfield."

"You won't get into trouble, don't worry," Lucky said, without knowing if this were actually true.

But now she had a major problem named Miles to worry about. Running away is one thing. Running away with a one-shoed five-year-old is much, much more complicated and dreadful.

19. eggs and beans

The windstorm seemed to be getting dis-*couraged* at last. It was less noisy, and you could see parts of blue sky through the dust. Lucky hoped strongly that the storm would blow way out into the desert that stretched before them like an ocean. From their protected spot in front of the dugout, the desert was all they could see. Hard Pan was far, far behind them.

HMS Beagle raised her head, her black nose twitching, when Miles began making the *where-are-you, where-are-you, where-are-you* call of a quail. Lucky let him. Being around Miles took a lot of energy, and she didn't have much left.

Suddenly Miles quit. He lay facedown on the towel and began to cry softly. Lucky sighed.

"Time for dinner," she said in her brisk nurse voice. As expected, Miles sat up and looked interested.

"I have sand in me everywhere," he announced. "Even under my clothes. What are we having?"

"First, hard-boiled eggs."

"Ewww. I only like eggs when the white part and the yellow part are mixed up together," Miles explained. "Can't we have scrambled eggs?"

"Do you see a stove around here? Do you see a fridge with fresh eggs inside? Do you see a *pan* for *cooking*?"

"No," said Miles in a small voice. "Is there any gravy? I love gravy for dinner."

"Beans," said Lucky in a don't-push-it, Brigitte-like way. She was saving the Fig Newtons for a later emergency. Maybe by breakfast time tomorrow Miles would decide to like hard-boiled eggs.

Miles peeped softly to himself while Lucky found the can, spoon, and little packets of ketchup. She was very hungry and thought how delicious the beans would taste.

But there was one problem, she realized.

No can opener.

"What's wrong?" Miles asked.

"Nothing. We're going to open our can just like the old miners who once lived in this dugout did, okay?" She had no idea how yet. Because of the look on his face, she said, "Miles, do you realize we're having a big adventure? This is going to be a *lot* of fun, but we also have to be *adaptable*, like Chesterfield and the other burros."

Miles still looked worried. "I can't run away overnight," he said. "I'm not allowed to."

Lucky decided to deal with that later. She peered into the cool darkness of the dugout. It smelled like ancient earth, like she imagined a tomb would smell, which was why she'd never explored in there before and did not want to go far inside now. She did not like that smell. But it wasn't too deep to see into the corners. A wooden crate held a jumble of old junk.

Checking first for the sticky, messy-looking web that black widows spin—not at all like Charlotte's beautiful flat web—Lucky searched for something she could use to get the lid off her can. There were a couple of sand-filled glass jars and bottles, a broken rake, a lot of rabbit droppings, and a rusty screwdriver.

She rubbed the screwdriver with sand to get off all the old germs and gunk, then wiped it with a corner of the towel. By holding the screwdriver at the rim of the can and pounding the handle with a rock, she made a small puncture. Steadying the can between her feet, she moved the screwdriver very slightly and made another puncture, widening the first one. She had to go almost all the way around before she could pry the spiky lid back.

"Okay, here's how the old miners do," Lucky said at last. She 119 tore off a corner of a ketchup packet, dipped the spoon in the can, poured a little ketchup on top, and ate the beans. "Yum," she said enthusiastically, to show Miles the one and only response she wanted to hear from him. She passed him the spoon and his own ketchup packet.

Miles dipped the spoon and squeezed a large dollop of ketchup on his hand, missing the spoon completely. Trying to lick it off his hand, he dumped the spoonful of beans on the towel. "Don't the old miners have a *plate*?" he asked.

"Too much trouble to wash up," Lucky said. She considered Plan B. "What you do," she said, "is you squirt ketchup straight on your tongue, then you eat a spoon of beans and it all swaps together in your mouth. Try it."

Miles did. By the time they slurped the last bean juice, taking turns, Miles had beans and ketchup in his hair and all over his T-shirt, but he hadn't cut  himself on the lid and he hadn't complained. He told Lucky she knew how to cook almost as good as Short Sammy.

As HMS Beagle finished her kibble and searched the ground for extra fallen morsels, Lucky was thinking that, considering the *horrendous* windstorm, the bother and trouble of Miles showing up, the cholla burr, and the lack of a can opener, still, all in all, it was a pretty successful Running-Away. She felt full and in charge. She looked grown up and maybe even pretty in Brigitte's dress.

It was then that Lucky felt a little fluttering in her ear and automatically slapped at it. She was not thinking about specimens because the sensation of something in your ear makes you forget all about Charles Darwin.

The bug in her ear went deeper. She tried to gouge it out with her finger but couldn't reach it. It got to a very deep place inside and sent a shooting, piercing pain into her head. She screamed and leaped to her feet, holding her head sideways. "Something crawled in my ear!" she screamed. "It's biting me!"

20. a good book

Lucky had always worried, in a far back corner of her mind that wasn't a scientific corner, about a bug crawling into her ear. This was partly why she had a garden-hedge perm. At night, if she remembered, she arranged a clump of hair over her ear, so any bug would come along and say, "Whoa, too hard to go through *that* thicket of hair," and find some other thing to do.

The main reason she had mineral oil in her survival kit was to smooth some on her eyebrows for glistening. But another use she knew for the oil was to drown bugs.

"I can get it out like you got my cactus out!" shouted Miles. "Let me try!"

"No! Get me the plastic bottle of oil, quick!" Lucky kept her head to the side in case the bug might fall out because of gravity, but instead it dug around deeper inside. Lucky never knew you could feel that much pain.

She had an urgent, tremendous bad scary feeling and a crazed panic, with that bug moving around and biting tender, sensitive places that should never be touched ever by anything. Its scrabbling and scritching noises filled up her entire head, and those noises drummed out other, regular noises. She grabbed the bottle from Miles, got down on the towel on her side, and aimed for her ear. A large glop spilled onto her hair and neck and Lucky started crying because she thought she'd used it all up and wasted it. But there was still a little oil left that she carefully poured, knowing more by feel, now, where the opening to her ear was.

Lucky tried to soothe herself out of the panicky feeling by remembering that the bug would drown sooner or later without danger of the mineral oil seeping into her brain. You have to be patient. The main thing is if the bug is injured instead of being killed, it will never come out and you will have to go to the hospital where the doctor will use a special, horrible tool to reach in—and Lucky did not want to think about that special tool and what *it* would feel like.

Miles made some machine-gun noises and limped off down the hill, kicking sand with his one shoe. Lucky did not move. It's important to wait until the bug fully dies in the oil. She didn't know if it was working, because the bug still fluttered and crashed around.

"I'm going back now, Lucky," Miles called from the foot of the little hill. "I'll bring help so you don't die from the bug in your brain."

Lucky fought to keep from crying. "Miles, no! I'm okay! I won't die! Don't you want to see the bug come out?"

122

"No!"

"Don't you want a Fig Newton?"

A pause. Miles was probably thinking this over. "I better get help first," he said.

"But I need you, Miles! I need *you* to help me!"

"Help you do what?"

There were many more seconds now between bug movements. "Help me wait. I can't move, but I'm very bored. I brought a good book. Could you please read it to me?"

"I don't know how to read enough words yet."

"Miles, I know you can read this one. Come on, get it out of that plastic sack."

Lucky knew Miles thought she was trying to trick him. Slowly he limped back up to the camp. She heard him rummaging in the sack. The bug moved, but only a little.

"'A mother bird sat on her egg,'" Miles read, and sighed deeply, his voice full of wonder.

By the time Miles finished reading *Are You My Mother?* Lucky decided she could safely turn onto her other side and drain her ear.

"Will blood come out?" Miles asked.

"I doubt it," said Lucky, but she wondered too.

The storm seemed to have blown itself out, and the sun was moving toward the rim of the far-off mountains. Lucky closed her eyes.

"Why is my mother in jail?" Miles asked suddenly.

"She made a mistake, Miles."

"So she's really not taking care of her friend in Florida?"

"No." Lucky felt a whoosh as a glug of oil spilled out. She shook her head in case there was more.

"It's better that she's in jail," said Miles, "because that means she's not staying away from me on *purpose.*"

Lucky did not know what to say.

"She'll come back when she's finished being in jail," Miles continued, "but if I tell her about running away, will she be mad?"

"I'll tell her how brave you were about the cholla burr and how you read to me and everything," said Lucky.

She lifted her head and examined the towel. A tiny white

moth, smaller than a housefly, lay there. Lucky had expected a gigantic beetle. She smiled, the pain completely gone, and sat up. "She'll be proud of you," she said.

"Guess what, Lucky! Here comes Chesterfield!"

They both heard steps approaching in the calm silence. But it wasn't a burro who came around the side of the hill. It was Lincoln.

21. amazing grace

The sky was smeared with red as the sun dipped down behind the Coso Mountains.

"Hey," said Lincoln, "what's up?"

"Nothing much," said Lucky, arranging the skirt of Brigitte's dress attractively, as if this were a usual, boring day. She felt her hair. It was full of sand, mineral oil, and twigs.

Lincoln got out a string and began tying it into a knot.

"We are living like the old miners! We ran away!" yelled Miles.

"I know," said Lincoln. "So does everyone else. They searched everywhere in town and figured out you must be here. I'm sure they'll be here sooner or later."

"Are they very mad?"

"Pretty worried, I guess. Short Sammy kept telling Brigitte about all the times *he* ran away and how he turned out okay anyway. He was trying to calm her down, but I think he made it worse."

Miles asked, "How do they know we're out here?"

Lincoln shrugged. "Mrs. Prender said you were always

talking about some burro named Chesterfield that lived in the dugouts," he said.

Lucky sighed. "Want an egg?" she said.

"Only if it's hard-boiled."

Lucky thought how strange it was that some small things turned out just right, which was rare for big important things to do. As the sunset faded and faded and the sky darkened, she and Lincoln ate eggs, Miles got a Fig Newton, and HMS Beagle polished off a carrot. The feel of the air, soft and nearly still, was something you usually wouldn't even notice. But now, after the dust storm, it felt like a kindness, a special thoughtful anonymous gift.

After a while, the full moon roared up into the sky behind their hill. Lucky thought that the people on Earth were very, very lucky to have their exact moon. They could have gotten a little puny moon like some of the other planets, and that would have totally messed up the oceans and the tides. Or their moon could have been too close or too far away. Or they could have had *two* moons or even more, and everything about their life would have been different. Lucky was sure, both as a scientist and as a girl-speck looking for her Higher Power, that it wouldn't have been as good.

She was thinking how most people didn't appreciate the moon enough at all, how they really didn't give it much *serious thought*, when Lincoln said, "Well, here they come."

There were many vehicles bumping along the dirt road: Short Sammy's old Cadillac and Brigitte's Jeep and Dot's pickup and Mrs. Prender's VW and the Captain's van, and more following in their dust. They drove slowly, shouting "Lucky! Miles! Lucky! Miles!" out of the windows.

"We could hide," said Lincoln.

But Lucky didn't want to hide, and anyway Miles was already lurching down to the road, as excited as if they had won a game of hide-and-seek. She sat on a rock and gazed out at the desert. Maybe they would think she'd kidnapped Miles, and send her to a special school in L.A. for bad kids, and if they did she would *become* a bad kid. She saw herself in a room full of beds like in a jail, each bed with a bad kid in it. They would take away her specimen boxes and her survival kit. Instead of being a ward with her own private personal Guardian, she would become a Ward of the State. And you can't sit on the State's lap and the State doesn't hug you before bed. Probably she would die of sadness, Lucky thought, seeing herself under a gray sheet, her face turned to the wall.

Car doors were slamming and dozens of people were getting out and shouting and laboring up to their camp. The air was so warm and the moon was so bright it was almost like daylight, except more mysterious. Lucky got something out of her plastic bag and ducked into the shadows of the dugout where she could watch.

She had something important to do before she surrendered.

HMS Beagle ran joyfully around greeting each arrival, including several other dogs. Everyone was talking at once, asking questions and hugging Miles. From inside the dugout it sounded like the whole town was there. When Brigitte called her name from nearby, Lucky stepped out into the moonlight and, looking down, saw that the silky dress and the urn both reflected its light.

"Thank you for coming to this memorial service for my mother," Lucky said in a clear, strong voice, and everyone stopped talking and turned to her with surprised faces. She saw that Brigitte suddenly had tears in her eyes.

Lucky was not sure what should happen next, and then she remembered the one thing her father—the man she'd thought was a crematory man—had said to her. He'd said that the decision she made would be the right one.

"These are her remains," Lucky went on, clutching the urn to her chest. The sense of her mother's smooth shoulder flooded her with sadness, and then Brigitte smiled up at her and clasped her hands under her chin, almost like praying.

As Lucky opened the lid of the urn, Short Sammy cleared his throat and began to sing "Amazing Grace." Dot's high, clean voice joined

in, and then everyone was singing, their voices clear and ringing in the still night.

Suddenly a breeze came, a little afterthought of the storm, as if, Lucky thought, some Higher Power was paying attention and knew what was needed. She walked to the edge of the ring of people and flung the remains of her mother up into the air, and everyone watched, singing, as the breeze lifted and carried them out into the great waiting desert.

22. *bonne nuit*

Lucky put on her summer nightgown, which was old and had become tight at the armholes. It was fresh and California soft from the dryer.

Brigitte came to the door. "Ready?" she asked, and sat on Lucky's bed.

Lucky was. Her hair was damp from a long shower that had rinsed off every speck of sand, grit, oil, and dust. She climbed onto Brigitte's lap, even though she was really much too big. But she still fit, and she leaned back while Brigitte wrapped her with her arms, like a present. Lucky felt sleepy and languid. Her knees were almost knobby enough to look like Brigitte's knees, though Lucky's were brown and scabby and scarred, and Brigitte's were beautiful and . . . Lucky searched for the word . . . womanly. From the floor where she lay, HMS Beagle touched her nose to Lucky's bare foot.

"So the papers in the suitcase are to take to the judge in Independence?" Lucky asked.

"Of course, *ma puce.* We need to show him your birth

certificate and my green card for living in California and all of that so I can legally adopt you."

"And," Lucky stretched back into Brigitte, feeling as if she'd come to the end of a long and difficult journey. "And the restaurant management course—that's to open a café in Hard Pan?"

"With a loan from your father, yes. What did you think, that I was going back to France?"

"Mmmm."

"Oh, Lucky," said Brigitte, and sighed.

After a moment Lucky said, "Brigitte, what is a scrotum?"

"It is a little sack of the man or the animal which has in it the sperm to make a baby," said Brigitte in her deep, quiet voice.

"Why do you ask about that?"

"It was just something I heard someone say," said Lucky.

For some reason, Brigitte said, "You know if anyone ever hurt you I would rip their heart out."

"I know," said Lucky, and she did. Tears came welling up behind her eyes for a second, then they went back inside for some other time, a sad time. A certain crevice of Lucky's mind wondered if there is some kind of reservoir for tears where they are stored, because sometimes there are so many of them, pouring and pouring out. Lucky leaned her head back and breathed in the sunscreen smell of Brigitte.

She got the back of her throat ready to say good night, and in drowsy, perfect French she said, "*Bonne nuit*, Brigitte."

Through her curly wedge of hair, Lucky felt the smile on Brigitte's cheek.

23. by and by

Lucky raked the patio in front of the Found Object Wind Chime Museum and Visitor Center. There was much less litter now that Brigitte's Hard Pan Café had opened for business. People went before and after the anonymous twelve-step meetings to get a piece of apple pie or a ham-and-cheese sandwich, which Brigitte wrote on the blackboard menu as *tarte aux pommes* and *croque-monsieur*, and pretty soon the geologists and tourists and everyone in the town knew how to say a lot of French words.

Once in a while, Brigitte put out a platter called "Commodity Tasting," cooked from the free Government food, and people helped themselves. Usually she added garlic and herbs and spices to make it taste better, and Lucky had the job of sprinkling the platter with parsley.

Lucky twisted shut the top of the black plastic trash bag and hauled it to the Dumpster in back. She inspected the place where the hole in the wall of the Found Object Wind Chime Museum and Visitor Center had been. She had plugged it up with Fix-All.

Not a sound emerged from inside.

She had done a good job.

acknowledgments

The author is deeply grateful to the following people for their advice, expertise, and support:

- My friends and colleagues at the Los Angeles Public Library. LAPL has been a second home to me almost my entire life, as well as a life-support system. Its staff is the best in the world.

- Priscilla (Moxom) White, whose courage and integrity are unparalleled in this universe.

- For their thoughtful reading of the first draft, deep thanks to Eva Cox, Nadia and Eva Mitnick, Erin Miskey, and Georgia Chun.

- Dr. Steven Chun, for invaluable pediatric advice.

- Patricia and David Leavengood, for extraordinary generosity.

- Jean-Marie and Aglaë Chance, *nos très grands amis.*

- Suzanne Cuperly *et* Liliane Moussy, *chère belle-sœur.*

- Myriam Lemarchand, *qui m'a fait comprendre tant de choses.*

- Joe and Jody Bruce, whose stories ignited this one.

- Lindsey Philpott, of the Pacific Americas Branch of the International Guild of Knot Tyers, for crucial technical support, and the Guild itself.

- Virginia Walter and Theresa Nelson, charter members with me of the DJ Fan Club. And warm thanks to Amy Kellman, whose encouragement helped me pitch the story.

- Susan Cohen, my kind, protocol-proof, good-humored agent.

- Matt Phelan, for giving these pictures such tender life and immediacy.

- Richard Jackson, dear world-class editor, for everything, but especially for having so much faith all these years.

- The Nortap clan: Sir Nigel, Beauregard, and my beloved Ernie.

to the reader

The book Ms. McBeam reads to Lucky's class is *The Tree of Life* by Peter Sis (Farrar, Straus and Giroux, 2003).

The book Miles reads, *Are You My Mother?* was written and illustrated by P. D. Eastman (Random House, 1960).

The website for the International Guild of Knot Tyers is www.igkt.net.

This is the little prayer that Lucky hears at the twelve-step meetings:

> *God grant us the serenity to accept the things we cannot change,*
> *Courage to change the things we can,*
> *And the wisdom to know the difference.*